THE TALKING PARCEL

Gerald Durrell is one of the few people who has managed to realize his childhood ambition. He has his own Zoo on the island of Jersey. He goes all over the world on collecting trips to find animals for his Zoo. He has concerned himself especially with wild-life preservation: many of the animals in Jersey Zoo would be nearly extinct were it not for his efforts. In addition to his Zoo activities, Gerald Durrell has written many humorous books, both for adults and children, about his experiences with animals.

'Gerald Durrell's knowledge of real animal behaviour and his obvious delight in mythological creatures are combined in this adventure which can easily be enjoyed by boys and girls of nine to twelve years.'

Children's Book Review

'Gerald Durrell possesses a quite extraordinary ability to make people laugh.'

The Times Literary Supplement

Gerald Durrell

THE TALKING PARCEL

april 1979.

*To new adventures
and lingering
memories*

*With Love
Deb*

FONTANA · LIONS

First Published 1974 by William Collins Sons and Co Ltd
14 St James's Place, London sw1
First published in Lions 1976
Second Impression January 1978

Made and printed in Great Britain by
William Collins Sons and Co Ltd Glasgow

CONTENTS

This book is for my God-daughter
Deirdre Alexandra Platt

Dear Deirdre,

Here is the book that I promised you and I hope you will enjoy it.

It is no good your asking me the next time we meet whether it is all true, because I have been sworn to secrecy. But I can give you some hints.

For example, I can tell you that Parrot's cousin in India was a very real bird and not only travelled in Rolls-Royces but had an International Passport as well. If at some time in the future you are in Greece, you will find Madame Hortense sitting on a siding exactly as I have described, and you will be able to take a diesel train up the valley to the very entrance of Mythologia. Finally, if you look in a book called *The History of Four-footed Beasts* by Edward Topsell, you will find that weasels were, in fact, the cure for Cockatrices.

As all these are true, how could you possibly disbelieve the rest?

Your loving Godfather,

GERRY

one

THE TALKING PARCEL

When Simon and Peter landed at Athens, to stay with their cousin Penelope, and the doors of the plane were opened, the heat hit them like a warm wave from an oven, and the brilliant sunshine made them screw up their eyes. After the generally soggy and grey weather they were used to in England, it was simply splendid, and the boys stretched and blinked with half-closed eyes, like cats in front of a fire, listening entranced to the crackle and pop of the Greek language being spoken all round them.

At first sight, Uncle Henry was a bit of a shock, for he was rather large, like a big, brown eagle, with a swooping nose and mane of white hair and enormous hands which he waved about incessantly. They wondered how on earth anyone who looked like Uncle Henry could be the father of someone as pretty as Penelope, for she was very slender with huge, green eyes and chestnut coloured hair.

"Ah," said Uncle Henry, glaring at them ferociously, "so you've arrived, eh? Good, good. Glad to see you. Glad to see that you're a little less repulsive than you were when I *last* saw you – just after you were born. You looked like a couple of baby white mice, all pink and horrible."

"Daddy," said Penelope, "don't be rude."

"Rude, rude?" said Uncle Henry, "I'm not being rude, just telling them."

"Is that your luggage over there?" asked Penelope.

"Yes," said Peter, "those two cases and the boat."

"Boat?" said Uncle Henry. "What boat?"

"It's a collapsible dinghy," Simon explained. "Dad bought it for us."

"What a very *sensible* thing to bring," said Uncle Henry. "How very *intelligent* of you both."

The boys glowed with pleasure and decided that perhaps Uncle Henry was not so bad, after all. When they had collected their luggage, they piled it into the boot of Uncle Henry's big, open car, and then they drove off in the hot sunshine through a landscape that soon became dotted with silvery olive trees and dark green cypress trees standing like spear-blades against the blue sky.

Uncle Henry's villa was a large, rambling house, set in the hills above the blue sea, and its wide verandas were shaded by vines heavy with the biggest bunches of grapes that the boys had ever seen. The house had white walls and huge, green shutters which, when half-closed, turned the rooms cool, dim and as green as an aquarium. The boys' room was enormous, with a tiled floor and a french window leading out on to the vine-covered veranda.

"Wow," said Peter, appreciatively, "I'll be able to pluck a bunch of grapes every morning before breakfast."

"And there are oranges and tangerines and figs in the garden," said Penelope, "and water melons, apricots and peaches." She sat on one of the beds, watching them as they unpacked.

"I can't really believe we are here yet," said Simon.

"Neither can I," said Peter, "except that it's so *hot*, so it must be real."

Penelope laughed. "It gets much hotter than this."

"Swimming, that's the answer," said Peter.

"That's what I thought we'd do this afternoon," said Penelope.

"After lunch. There's a *huge* beach just below us here, and it's marvellous swimming."

"And we can launch the dinghy," said Simon.

"Wonderful," said Peter. "We'll go on a voyage of discovery."

So, when they'd finished lunch, the three children changed into their bathing costumes and took the dinghy and its pump, and made their way down the stony hillside, that smelt deliciously of thyme and myrtle, to where the great dazzling white beach stretched away in each direction as far as the eye could see. The blue waters were as still as a lake and as transparent as glass. It was hot work pumping up the dinghy: and the children had to keep stopping to have a cooling dip in the sea before continuing. But at last it was pumped up, and it floated fatly in the shallow water, like a plump blue cloud. They scrambled aboard, taking with them the essentials of travel that Penelope had insisted they bring: a large beach umbrella and a bag containing some lemonade. Then, with Simon and Peter rowing and Penelope steering, they set off down the coast. The sun beat down on them and from the shore they could hear the faint zithering cries of the cicadas in the olive trees. After they had progressed a quarter of a mile or so the boys paused in their rowing and wiped the sweat from their faces.

"It's jolly hot work," said Peter.

"Yes," agreed Simon. "I'm simply roasting."

"Perhaps we've gone far enough," said Penelope. "After all, it is your first day and it *is* hot. Why don't we make camp somewhere?"

Simon glanced over his shoulder. A few hundred yards away a long, low sandbank stuck out from the beach, forming a tiny bay. "How about there?" he suggested. "Let's anchor there, by the sandbank."

They rowed into the tiny bay and anchored the dinghy

in the still waters, and then they put up the umbrella (which cast a patch of shade the size of a mushroom) and Penelope opened three bottles of lemonade. Grateful for the patch of shade, they lay there and drank the lemonade thirstily. Then, drugged by the heat and exhausted by their rowing, the two boys fell asleep, their heads pillowed on their arms. Penelope finished her lemonade and dozed for a while, and then decided to climb to the top of the sand dune and see what the next stretch of beach looked like. The sand was almost too hot to walk on, but she reached the top of the dune and ahead the beach stretched to the horizon it seemed, but in the distance it was so shimmering with heat haze she couldn't really make anything out. She was just about to return to the welcome shade of the umbrella when she noticed the thing in the water.

At first, she thought it was a log of wood, but it was too fat for that even without branches. It was floating shoreward, propelled by tiny ripples created by a baby breeze that had sprung up. Gradually, it was washed in on to the shore just below where Penelope stood, and she could see it was a large, brown paper parcel tied with purple cord. It came to rest on the shore, and she was just going to run down the sand dune and investigate, when the parcel spoke.

"What ho," said the parcel, in a squeaky sort of voice. "What ho, land ho! by Jove, and about time too. All this upsy-downsy, upsy-downsy stuff is detrimental to my innards."

Penelope stared down at the parcel, disbelievingly. It looked like a large, perfectly ordinary, brown paper parcel tied up with purple cord, standing about three feet high and measuring some two feet across. It was vaguely in the shape of an old-fashioned beehive.

"Sea-sickness is a scourge," the parcel went on. "My

great grandmother suffered so much from it that she was frequently sea-sick while having a bath."

"Who on earth is it talking to?" thought Penelope. "It can't be talking to me."

Just at that moment another voice came from the parcel. A faint, sweet, tinkling voice, like the echo of a sheep bell. "Oh, do shut up about your grandmother and sea-sickness," it said irritably. "I'm just as sick as you. What I want to know is, what we do now?"

"We have arrived," said the squeaky, first voice, "thanks to my brilliant navigation. Now we wait to be rescued."

The parcel, Penelope had decided, was much too small to contain a human being, let alone two human beings, and yet there were undeniably two voices coming from it. The whole thing was very creepy, and Penelope felt that she would feel happier if she had Peter and Simon to help solve this mystery with her, so, turning, she ran down the dune towards the umbrella where the boys were sleeping, blissfully unconscious of the adventure that was just starting.

'Peter, Simon, wake up, wake up,' hissed Penelope, in a whisper, shaking the boys. "*Wake up*, it's very important."

"What's the matter," asked Simon, sitting up and yawning sleepily.

"Tell her to go away," mumbled Peter. "Want to sleep, too hot for playing games."

"I'm *not* playing games," whispered Penelope indignantly. "You must wake up. I've found something most peculiar on the other side of the sandbank."

"What have you found?" asked Simon, stretching himself.

"A parcel," said Penelope. "A large parcel."

"Good heavens," groaned Peter. "Is that all you've woken us up for?"

"What's so unusual about a parcel?" asked Simon.

"Have you ever found a parcel that *talks*?" asked

Penelope, sarcastically. "It's not the sort of thing that's happened to me very often."

"Talks?" spluttered Peter, wide awake now. "*Talks?* You must be imagining things. You've got sunstroke."

"A talking parcel?" said Simon. "You must be joking."

"I'm not joking, neither have I got sunstroke," said Penelope angrily. "And what's more it talks in two voices."

The boys stared at her. She was obviously not joking, and equally obviously she had not got sunstroke. "I say, Penny," said Simon uneasily, "are you sure you are not imagining things?"

Penelope stamped with vexation. "Of course I'm not," she whispered vehemently. "You're both so *stupid*. It's a parcel with two voices and it's talking to itself. If you don't believe me, come and see."

Rather reluctantly, for they still felt that Penelope might be pulling their legs, the boys followed her up the sand dune. When they reached the top, she put a finger to her lips and said: "Sh . . ." Then she lay down on her tummy and crawled the rest of the way. Presently three heads: one blond, one dark and one copper-coloured peered over the top of the dune. At the base of the dune lay the parcel. Tiny wavelets were breaking around it, and the boys stared in amazement, for the parcel had now started to sing to itself in two separate voices.

> Moon carrot Pie, Moon carrot Pie
> It'll liven you up, bring a gleam to your eye.
> Oh, a cow in a manger, a pig in a sty
> They all love their slices of
> Moon carrot Pie.
>
> Moon carrot Tart, Moon carrot Tart
> It'll stir up your blood, and give strength to your heart.
> The donkey, the pony, the horse with its cart
> They all love to munch at their
> Moon carrot Tart.

> Moon carrot Stew, Moon carrot Stew
> There's nothing quite like it, from all points of view.
> The pigeon and turkey, to name but a few
> Just cannot get on without
> Moon carrot Stew.

"There you are," whispered Penelope, triumphantly "What did I tell you."

"It's incredible," said Peter. "What do you think it is? A couple of dwarfs?"

"They would have to be very small dwarfs to fit in that," said Penelope.

"Well, we can't tell *what* it is," said Simon, practically, "until we unwrap it."

"How do you know it will *like* being unwrapped?" asked Peter, thoughtfully.

"It did say something about being rescued," said Penelope.

"Well, we'll ask it," said Simon. "At least it speaks English." He strode down the sand dune, followed by the others, and approached the parcel which sang on, oblivious to his presence.

> Moon carrot Jam, Moon carrot Jam
> It's really so good, it's made me what I am.
> The man of a hundred, the babe in its pram
> They can't get along without
> Moon carrot Jam.

Simon cleared his throat. "Excuse me," he said, "I'm sorry to interrupt but . . ."

> Moon carrot Soup, Moon carrot Soup
> It's the stuff you must drink when you're starting to droop.
> The duck in the duckpond, the hens in their coop
> They're regular gluttons for
> Moon carrot Soup.

"Excuse me," said Simon again, very much more loudly.

There was silence, as the parcel stopped singing.

"What was that?" asked the tinkly voice at last, in a faint, frightened whisper.

"A voice," said the squeaky voice. "I'm almost certain it was a voice, unless, of course, it was a thunderstorm or a typhoon or a tidal wave, or maybe an earthquake, or . . ."

"EXCUSE ME!" said Simon, very loudly this time, "but do you want to be unwrapped?"

"There," said the squeaky voice, "I told you it was a voice. A voice offering to unwrap us. How *kind*. Shall we say 'Yes'?"

"Oh yes," said the tinkly voice. "We've been in the dark so long."

"Very well," said the squeaky voice. "We will allow you to unwrap us."

The children gathered round the parcel and Simon pulled out his penknife and carefully cut the thick, purple string that bound it, and then they started to unwrap the paper.

When the children had pulled off the paper, they found underneath what appeared to be a huge, quilted tea-cosy, heavily embroidered with gold thread in a pattern of leaves and flowers.

"Um, do you want us to take off your er, your er . . . tea-cosy?" asked Simon.

"Tea-cosy?" asked the squeaky voice, indignantly. "Tea-cosy, you ignorant voice? That's not a *tea-cosy*. It's a covering against night winds and inclement weather, made out of genuine, rainbow caterpillar silk, that is."

"Oh," said Simon, "I'm sorry. Well, whatever it is, would you like us to remove it?"

"Of course," said the squeaky voice. "Spare no effort to make this rescue a successful one."

At the top of the tea-cosy was a sort of plaited loop, and taking hold of this Simon lifted off the whole covering. Underneath was a large, domed golden cage, but it was totally unlike any other cage the children had ever seen, for it was furnished with extremely elegant miniature furniture. Apart from two cedar-wood perches and a swing, there was a handsome four-poster bed with red velvet curtains, covered with a beautifully sewn patch-work bedspread made out of the tiniest scraps of multi-coloured silks and damasks, and a small Louis Quinze dining table and chair, and an elegant glass-fronted cabinet full of beautiful hand-painted china. Then there was a full-length gilt-edged mirror with an ivory brush and comb hanging by it, and a very comfortable chaise-longue upholstered in royal blue velvet, and beside it a rosewood harpsichord.

Sitting at ease on the chaise-longue was the most extraordinary parrot the children had ever seen. His plumage was purple and gold and green and blue and pink, glittering and gleaming and shifting like an opal. He had a great, smooth, curved beak – so black that it looked as if it had been carved from coal – and eyes the colour of periwinkles. But the most surprising thing about the parrot was its feathering, for, instead of lying smooth, each feather was stuck up and curled round, like the fur of a poodle. This gave him the look of a strange-coloured tree in spring when its buds are just bursting. He was wearing a green silk skull cap with a long, black silk tassel. Next to the chaise-longue on which the parrot was reclining was a small table, and on it was another cage – but a tiny one, the size of a thimble, and in it sat a glittering, golden spider, with a jade-green cross on its back. It was obvious that the tinkly voice belonged to the spider, and that the squeaky voice belonged to the parrot.

"So *that's* what it is," said Peter.

"It?" said the parrot, sitting up indignantly. "*It?*"

"A parrot!" said Penelope, delighted.

"It was just a parrot, an ordinary, talking parrot," said Simon.

"Why didn't we think of that?"

"NOW LOOK HERE!" said the parrot, so loudly and fiercely that the children stopped talking.

"Now look here," it went on in a lower tone of voice, having got their attention. "Let's have a tiny bit less of this '*A*' parrot stuff, shall we?"

"I'm sorry," said Penelope. "We didn't mean to offend you."

"Well, you did," said the parrot.

"But you *are* a parrot, aren't you?" asked Peter.

"Now, there you go again," said the parrot angrily. "All this screechy-weachy stuff about a parrot. I'm not *a* parrot, I'm THE parrot."

"I'm sorry, I don't think we understand you," said Penelope, puzzled.

"Anyone, or rather any parrot, can be *a* parrot," the parrot explained, "but I'm *the* Parrot. The initials alone should have told you."

"Initials? What initials?" asked Simon, bewildered.

"Mine," said the parrot. "You really do ask the most ridiculous sort of questions."

"But what initials?" asked Penelope.

"Work them out for yourself," said the parrot. "My names are Percival, Archibald, Reginald, Roderick, Oscar, Theophilus."

"Why, that spells 'parrot'," said Penelope, delightedly. "What lovely initials."

"Thank you," said the parrot, modestly. "That is why I am not *a* parrot. I'm *the* Parrot. You may call me Parrot."

"Thank you," said Penelope.

"This, here," he continued gesturing to the small cage with his wing, "is Dulcibelle, my singing spider."

"How do you do," said the children.

"How do you do," said Dulcibelle.

"How do you do," said Parrot.

"I must say," said Penelope, thoughtfully, "I can see why you are *the* Parrot. I mean I don't want to be rude, or anything, but you talk much better than most parrots. I mean, more intelligently, if you know what I mean. I mean, you seem to know what you're talking about, which most parrots *don't*."

"Of course," said Parrot. "And d'you know why most parrots don't know what they're talking about?"

"Why?" said Simon.

"Because they're taught by humans," said Parrot. "A most reprehensible way of learning."

"Well, how did you learn?" asked Peter.

"I was taught by the dictionary," said Parrot, proudly.

"By a dictionary?" said Penelope, incredulously. "How can you be taught by a dictionary?"

"How else?" inquired Parrot. "The trouble with most, if not all parrots, is, as I say, that they're taught by humans – that's why they don't know what they're saying, because the humans never explain to them what they're teaching them."

"I never thought of that," said Peter.

"What sane, healthy, normal, intelligent, self-respecting parrot would go round all day, saying 'Pretty Polly', if he knew what it meant?" asked Parrot, in a voice shaken with passion. "What decent, honest, shy, retiring, modest bird would go round inviting complete strangers to 'scratch Poll', if he knew what it *meant*?"

"When you put it like that, it seems almost like cruelty," said Penelope, thoughtfully.

"Yes," agreed Simon, "like the awful things they teach to babies – 'Dada, Mama, Bow-wow,' and so on."

"Exactly," said Parrot, triumphantly. "Now, what normal baby would go round, addressing every member of the ungulates he met as 'Moo-Moo', if he knew what it meant?"

"Every member of the what?" asked Peter.

"He means cows," said Simon, who was cleverer at long words than Peter.

"No, no," Parrot went on, "the only way to learn to speak is to be taught by a dictionary, and I was extremely lucky that I was brought up by a large, kindly and comprehensive dictionary, in fact, *The* Dictionary."

"How can you be brought up by a dictionary?" asked Penelope, puzzled.

"Where I come from, you can," said Parrot. "The Dictionary is the most human book in the place, next to the Great Book of Spells and Hepsibar's Herbal."

"I'm afraid I don't understand," said Penelope.

"You are a singularly obtuse, obdurate, sort of a girl," said Parrot, "besides being inconsequential, incomprehensible and incoherent."

"I don't think there is any need for you to start being rude again," said Peter, who hadn't understood half the words, but did not like the sound of them, and felt he ought to defend his cousin.

"Rude?" said Parrot. "*Rude?* I'm not being rude, just merely giving some words an airing, poor little things. Part of my job."

"Giving *words* an airing?" asked Simon. "How can you?"

"He's the Keeper of the Words," said Dulcibelle suddenly, in her tinkly, little voice. "It's a very important job."

"When we require interruption from you, we shall ask for it," said Parrot, eyeing Dulcibelle severely.

"I'm sorry," said Dulcibelle, bursting into tears. "I was only trying to help; only trying to give credit where credit was due; only trying to . . ."

"Will you *shut up*?" roared Parrot.

"Oh, very well," said Dulcibelle, retreating to the back of her cage, and starting to powder her nose. "I shall sulk."

"Sulk," said Parrot, "typical of a female spider."

"What's all this about giving words an airing?" asked Simon.

"What does 'Keeper of the Words' mean?" asked Peter.

"Well," said Parrot, "it's quite true, but you mustn't let it go any further. You see, where we come from, we have three books which govern our lives. They're talking books, of course, not like your dull, old, everyday books. One is the Great Book of Spells, the other is Hepsibar's Herbal, and the third is the Giant Dictionary. I was brought up by the Dictionary, so therefore I became Keeper of the Words."

"And what does that mean?" asked Penelope.

"Ah," said Parrot. "It's a very important job, I can tell you. Do you know how many words there are in the English language?"

"No," said Penelope.

"Hundreds," said Peter.

"More like thousands," said Simon.

"Quite right," said Parrot. "To be exact, two hundred thousand words. Now the average person uses the same words day after day, day in and day out." Here, his eyes filled with tears and he pulled out a large, spotted handkerchief from under his wing and blew his beak.

"So," he went on, his voice shaken with sobs. "What do you think happens to all the words that aren't used?"

"What happens to them?" asked Penelope, wide-eyed.

"If they're not looked after and given exercise, they simply fade away and vanish, poor little things," said Parrot. "That's my job. Once a year I have to sit down and recite the Dictionary, to make sure that all the words get the correct amount of exercise, but during the course of the year I try to use as many as possible because, really, one outing a year is not enough for the little fellows. They get so bored, sitting there between the pages."

"Time is getting on," said Dulcibelle suddenly.

"I thought you were sulking?" said Parrot, glaring at her.

"I've finished," said Dulcibelle. "It was a lovely sulk, but time's getting on."

"What do you mean, time's getting on?" said Parrot irritably.

"Well, we don't want just to sit here all day while you give us lectures on words," said the spider. "It's time we were getting back. Remember we've a lot to do."

"*We* have a lot to do; *we* have a lot to do, I like that," said Parrot angrily. "All *you* do all day is to sit in your cage and sing and sulk, and it's left to me to master-mind everything, to make the major decisions, to give that masterly display of courage and cunning . . ."

"I don't think it's very cunning to get us both exiled," interrupted Dulcibelle, sniffing. "Not what I would call cunning, anyway."

"That's right, that's right, blame *me*," shouted Parrot. "How was I to know they'd attack in the night, eh? How was I to know that the Toads would tie us up in a vulgar, brown paper parcel and throw us in the river, eh? You'd think, the way you go on, I'd encouraged the Cockatrices to take over, you . . . you . . . stupid, superannuated, singing spider, you . . ."

"I shall sulk," screamed Dulcibelle, starting to sob. "I shall sulk for *an hour*. Our contract does not allow you to insult me more than once a week, and you've done it *twice* today."

"Oh, all right, all right," said Parrot, in a harassed tone of voice. "I'm sorry; here, stop sulking and I'll give you a blue-bottle pasty when we get back."

"Promise?" asked Dulcibelle.

"Yes, yes, I promise," said Parrot irritably.

"You wouldn't like to make it a blue-bottle pasty *and* a grasshopper soufflé?" asked Dulcibelle wheedlingly.

"No, I wouldn't," said Parrot shortly.

"Oh, well," sighed Dulcibelle, and started to powder her nose again, humming softly to herself.

"What's all this about Toads?" asked Peter, in astonishment.

"And Cockatrices," said Penelope. "What are they?"

"What have they taken over?" asked Simon.

"And why are you exiled?" asked Penelope.

"Quiet," shouted Parrot, "quiet, quiet, *quiet*."

The children sat silent.

"Now," said Parrot. "Will you first of all please undo the door?"

Hastily Simon took out his penknife and cut the purple string that tied up the door, and then opened it.

"Thank you," said Parrot, stepping out and climbing on top of the cage.

"Mind you don't catch a chill out there," shouted Dulcibelle. "You haven't got your cloak on."

Parrot ignored her. He carefully adjusted his skull-cap, which had got pushed lop-sidedly over one eye during his climb, and surveyed the children.

"Now," he said at last. "You want to know the answers to all these questions, eh?"

"Yes, please," said Penelope.

"Can I trust you?" asked Parrot.

"Of course you can," said Simon, indignantly.

"Well then," said Parrot. "What I'm about to tell you is a strict secret, understand? Not a word to anyone else."

The children promised faithfully that everything Parrot told them would go no further, and settled down, round the cage, to listen.

two

TRAIN TO MYTHOLOGIA

"Well," said Parrot, "it was around the year when Hengist Hannibal Junketberry finished his magicianship. Being the seventh son of a seventh son of a seventh son, he had, not unnaturally, passed out top of his class and received among other honours the Merlin Award."

"Is that the best you can get?" asked Penelope.

"It means you're almost as good a magician as Merlin, and he was the best. Now at the time when Hengist Hannibal left the University of Magic with his prize (which consisted of the three books I've already mentioned, and a pointed hat and a magic wand) his old teacher begged him to specialise in something and make a name for himself. The country was too full of third-rate magicians, all mumbling the same old spells, and Hengist Hannibal's teacher thought that – with his talents – he should go far. Well, after some thought, he decided to take up mythological animals, because no one was doing them in those days."

"What's a mythological animal?" whispered Penelope to Simon.

"An imaginary one, like a sea serpent," Simon whispered back.

"Very soon," Parrot went on, "if anyone wanted to know how many toes a dragon had or how long a mermaid's hair was, they automatically went to Hengist Hannibal Junketberry, as he was *the* authority on the subject. In fact a lot of the information in Topsell's History of Four-footed Beasts came from Junketberry, but Topsell didn't give him the credit. Professional jealousy – that's what." Parrot paused, reached under his wing and took out a tiny, gold snuffbox, took a pinch of snuff and sneezed violently into his spotted handkerchief.

"I told you you'd catch cold without your cloak," shouted Dulcibelle, angrily. "Why don't you use your commonsense?"

Parrot ignored her. "After a few years, however," he continued, "Hengist Hannibal suddenly found his trade dropping off, if I may put it like that. He found that people were no longer coming to him for a unicorn's horn or a phial full of phoenix ashes against lightning. And the reason for this, he soon discovered, was that people were no longer believing."

Parrot paused and gazed at them sternly.

"I don't understand," said Simon, frowning. "If the animals were mythological in the first place, they didn't exist."

"Foolish boy," said Parrot. "They existed when people *believed* in them."

"I don't see how a thing can exist simply because you believe in it," said Simon stubbornly.

"Not just you, a whole lot of people," said Parrot. "Look, at one time, nobody believed in steam engines or paddle steamers, right? So there weren't any and then a lot of people started believing in steam engines and paddle steamers, and . . . bang . . ."

"Thunder," shouted Dulcibelle.

"Soon there were so many steam engines and paddle steamers you could hardly move. Well, it was the same with mythological animals," said Parrot. "As long as enough people believed in them, there were plenty of animals, but as soon as people started disbelieving in them, then . . . bang . . . their population dwindled away."

"That's two claps of thunder, I've heard," shouted Dulcibelle. "Come in, or you'll be struck by lightning."

"Oh, do be quiet," said Parrot impatiently. "Why don't you go and spin yourself something?"

"What?" asked Dulcibelle.

"Oh, anything," said Parrot.

"I'll spin a wimple," said Dulcibelle. "I've always wanted a wimple."

"Things soon became so bad," continued Parrot, "that Hengist Hannibal was at his wits' end: unicorns down to the last four pairs, sea serpents you couldn't find for love or money – it was terrible, simply because nobody believed any more."

"What did Mr Junketberry do?" asked Penelope, fascinated.

Parrot looked round carefully to make sure that they were not overheard and he put a wing up to his beak. "He created a country called Mythologia," said Parrot in a hoarse whisper.

"But where is it?" asked Penelope.

"And how did that solve everything?" asked Peter.

"Wait, wait, *wait*," said Parrot. "All in good time."

"You haven't seen my spinning pattern for a wimple, have you?" shouted Dulcibelle.

"No," said Parrot fiercely, "I have *not*." He paced up and down on the top of the cage for a while, wings behind his back, and then he stopped.

"Well, Hengist Hannibal found Mythologia quite by accident one day. He was walking in the hills and he came to this cave. Entering it, out of curiosity, he found it led him to a gigantic cavern under the earth, with a vast inland sea dotted with numerous islands. Immediately he could see that this was exactly what was wanted. After all, the world was fast becoming so disbelieving and so overcrowded there was scarcely any room left for real animals, let alone mythological ones. So he took it over and, with the aid of a few very potent spells, he made it most habitable, most habitable indeed. Then all the remaining mythological animals were moved down there, and each was given its own island or piece of sea, and everybody settled down most happily. You see, as long as we all believed in *each other* we were safe."

Parrot paused and wiped away a tear and blew his beak violently.

"I told you you'd catch cold," shouted Dulcibelle. "Do you listen to me? Oh, no!"

"Our Government, if you like to call it that," Parrot went on, "consisted of the three Talking Books, and Hengist Hannibal Junketberry, and a very good and fair and kind Government it was. As I've told you, I was made Keeper of the Words and part of my job was to come out into the real world once every hundred years or so and make a report of what was going on. Well, Dulcibelle and I have just been stopping with my cousin in India. He owns the Maharaja of Jaipur; you know, he's a terrible snob with an International Passport and a Rolls-Royce and everything, but he keeps me up-to-date on the Far Eastern situation. Anyway, we came back from this trip, and what do you think we found?"

The children waited, breathless.

"We found," said Parrot, in a deep, mournful and solemn voice, "that the Cockatrices had revolted. Not only that, but they'd stolen the three Talking Books of Government. Can you imagine anything more hideous, horrendous or horrifying?"

"No," said the children, truthfully, because tne way Parrot said it, it sounded just like the end of the world.

"Quite right," said Parrot, approvingly.

"But please," said Penelope, "before you go any further, can you please explain what a Cockatrice is?"

"Yes, please do, Parrot," said Simon and Peter.

"Well," said Parrot, "well, I must confess, though we in

Mythologia believe in live and let live, I must confess I've never *really* liked the Cockatrices: noisy, vulgar and vain – that more or less sums them up. Careless too, always breathing out fire and setting light to things – dangerous. What do they look like? Well, most unprepossessing, *I* think. They're about as big as you are with the body of a cockerel, the tail of a dragon, and instead of feathers they have scales. Of course, they're colourful with their red and gold and green scales, if you *like* that sort of thing. Personally, I think it's terribly brash and vulgar."

"But what do they breathe fire *for*?" asked Peter.

"I don't know really," said Parrot. "They were just thought up like that, but it's jolly dangerous, I can tell you. Hengist Hannibal was going to build them a special fire-proof castle to live in. The first one they had, they burnt down within twenty-four hours of moving into it. Now they're living in the Castle H.H. *used* to reside in before he moved up to the Crystal Caves, and I expect they'll burn *that* down eventually."

"Aren't they terribly dangerous creatures to have around?" asked Penelope.

"Not if you control their numbers," answered Parrot. "We never allowed more than ten dozen at any one time."

"But how do you manage to do that?" asked Simon.

"It was one of the Laws," said Parrot. "So many Unicorns, so many Mandrakes, so many Cockatrices, and so on. We had to, otherwise we'd have been overrun. There's only room for a certain amount of us in Mythologia, you see. Mind you, the Cockatrices are always trying to get their numbers up, always coming to H.H. with some story of having no one to do their washing. Well, it's all a bit complicated really. You see, Cockatrices are only hatched out of eggs laid by the two Golden Cockerels. They're dull birds, no conversation, just sit around saying cock-a-doodle-do in a fatuous manner all day. Well, once every hundred years, they'd lay an egg."

"But I thought only hens laid eggs?" said Penelope, confused.

"Hens lay eggs that hatch into other hens," corrected Parrot. "Golden Cockerels lay eggs that hatch into Cockatrices."

His answer so muddled Penelope that she decided not to ask any more questions.

"Once the Golden Cockerels have laid a Cockatrice's egg, then their job is done," explained Parrot. "They then let off a couple of boastful doodle-dos and hand the whole thing over to the Toads."

"The Toads?" said Penelope, now completely bewildered.

"What have Toads got to do with it?" asked Simon.

"They hatch the eggs, of course," said Parrot. "Only thing they're fit for, those Toads – brainless, dithering creatures. The only thing they do well is hatching Cockatrices' eggs. You know if you keep interrupting me like this, I'll never finish the story."

"Sorry," said the children, contritely, and fell silent.

"Well," said Parrot. "The Cockatrices decided that if they could get the great Book of Spells it would tell them how to make the Golden Cockerels lay a Cockatrice egg every day. So they got into league with the Toads, who are flibberty gibberty sort of creatures and easily led, and together they not only kidnapped the Golden Cockerels but stole the three Great Books of Government. When Dulcibelle and I returned, they'd locked themselves up in their castle and were producing Cockatrice eggs like a . . . like a . . . like a . . ."

"Battery farm," suggested Simon.

"Exactly," said Parrot. "Twenty-five eggs at the last count. One a day they're producing. The whole of Mythologia will be overrun with Cockatrices, unless we do something, or rather unless *I* do something. You see, over the last two hundred years or so, H.H. has become very frail and forgetful, and he's left more and more of the running of the thing to me. But I can't do anything without the Great Books. Dulcibelle and I were planning to go and try to talk some sense into the silly Cockatrices, but we were set upon in the middle of the night by those illiterate, ill-favoured and insolent Toads, bundled up into a vulgar, brown-paper parcel and thrown into the river. *Me*, Parrot! My blood boils at the thought. Wait until I get my wings on those Toads."

"But what about Mr Junketberry?" asked Penelope. "Poor man, what's happened to him?"

"He's in despair, poor fellow," said Parrot. "He was in his magician's cave with a hysterical Dragon on his hands, the last time I saw him."

"Dragon?" asked Peter, who was feeling a bit dazed with all these strange creatures.

"Tabitha, the last of the Dragons," explained Parrot. "Nice enough creature in her way but so useless. She let the Cockatrices have the eggs. When she realised what she'd done, of course, she had hysterics. No stamina, these Dragons."

"Don't you think you ought to get back as soon as possible?" asked Penelope anxiously. "I mean before all the Cockatrices hatch?"

"Exactly," said Parrot, "but I can't do it without help."

"We'll help," said Penelope eagerly. "We'll do anything, won't we, Peter . . . Simon?"

"Yes," chorused the boys, "anything, just tell us."

"You're too kind," said Parrot, wiping away a tear. "Too kind."

"In fact I wouldn't mind coming with you," said Peter, pugnaciously, "and helping you give those Cockatrices a good hiding."

"Yes," said Simon, "and those odious Toads."

"Couldn't we come back with you?" asked Penelope. "I mean we might be of some help."

"My dear young people," said Parrot, quite overcome with emotion. "You're too kind, too generous. Of course, you may come. I'd be most grateful for your help."

"Good," said Peter, jumping to his feet. "That's settled then. How do we get there?"

"By train," said Parrot.

"By *train*?" echoed the astonished children.

"Yes," said Parrot. "Originally, there was only a track up to our entrance. Then they put a train in – a narrow gauge, of course – round about eighteen hundred. Well, the track passed right by our entrance, so we had to let the train in on our secret, you see. She's French, but a very good sort. In fact, I've forgotten how to find this entrance myself. I generally use one of the others, but the train knows. She's retired now, of course, and lives at the village of Diakofta."

"But I've seen her, she's in our village. I mean the village nearest our villa," squeaked Penelope excitedly. "You mean that dear, little steam engine that stands on a sort of stage near the station?"

"That's right," said Parrot. "How's she looking?"

"Fine," said Penelope. "She's *sweet*."

"We never showed the diesel the entrance," said Parrot. "Untrustworthy things diesels, but old Madame Hortense is all right. They don't build them like that these days. If we go up there tonight, she'll take us to the entrance of Mythologia. From there we'll have to go on foot, following the river."

"If there's a river, why can't we go by boat?" asked Simon.

"Ah, we could, if only we had one," said Parrot.

"But we have," shouted Peter, triumphantly. "It's behind this sand dune."

"You're joking," said Parrot, faintly.

"No," said Penelope. "Go and look."

Parrot took off from the top of his golden cage and soared over the sand dune, glittering in the sun like a rainbow. He reappeared presently and landed again on top of his cage.

"You shouldn't be flying about like that at your age," shouted Dulcibelle. "I've told you before."

"Magnificent," said Parrot, breathlessly. "Magnificent, just what we needed: collapsible and such a beautiful colour, too. Children, I'm so glad we met."

"So are we," said Penelope.

"Now let's make plans," said Parrot. "What I suggest is this: if you'll be kind enough to conceal me and Dulcibelle in our cage up near the road somewhere, and then you can come back at midnight and we'll make our way to the village of Diakofta and persuade Madame Hortense to take us to the borders of Mythologia. From then on we can travel by boat. How does that strike you as a scrumptious plan?"

"Super," said Simon, grinning.

"Simon and I will be in charge of weapons and things," said Peter.

"And Penelope can be in charge of food and first-aid."

"Gosh," said Simon, struck by a thought. "How long is this going to take?"

"Several days, I would say," said Parrot. "Why?"

"What about your father, Penny?" asked Simon. "How are we going to explain to him?"

"That's easy," said Penelope. "He told me I could go and camp on the beach when you two arrived. We'll just tell him we're camping. Leave that to *me*."

"Well, that's settled. So let's get cracking," said Peter eagerly.

Carefully they carried Parrot's cage up the hill and concealed it not far from the road in a great cluster of myrtle bushes. Then they rowed back home, deflated the dinghy and carried it up to the villa. As Penelope had promised, Uncle Henry made no fuss about their going to camp on the beach.

"It's full moon," explained Penelope, "and we might spend several nights down there, so you're not to get worried."

"No, I sha'n't," said Uncle Henry. "I loved camping out at full moon when I was your age. Well, have a good time."

The three children went off to the boys' bedroom to pack up their supplies. Simon made them three spears by tying sharp kitchen knives to bamboos, and Peter made them catapults out of forked olive wood sticks and strong elastic that Penelope found. In addition, they had three torches, a compass, a first-aid box containing such things as plasters, bandages and cotton wool, and three large boxes of matches. Parrot had assured them that there would be plenty of food when they reached the Crystal Caves where H.H. lived. So they took only enough for twenty-four hours and only those things that didn't have to be cooked, like raisins and nuts and chocolate. Then they sat on the bed and waited for midnight.

As twelve o'clock struck, they crept out of the house and made their way down the moonlit road, carrying their weapons and supplies, and the all-important dinghy. When they reached the myrtle bushes where they had left Parrot, they saw a strange glow, as of a camp fire, and as they crept closer they saw that Parrot had lit two candles in the candelabra on his harpsichord and was playing a quiet, tinkly sort of tune, while Dulcibelle hummed to herself. It was such a pretty scene with the candle-light winking on the gold bars of the cage and the polished wood of the harpsichord and other furniture, the soft music and Dulcibelle's sweet, little voice, that the children were loath to disturb Parrot, but they felt they must.

"Ha, there you are," said Parrot when he saw them, ending the tune by running one wing-tip along the keyboard and closing the lid of the harpsichord. "Good, then we'll be off."

So, carrying Parrot's cage with Parrot sitting on top of it, the children set off for the village of Diakofta, which lay about a mile away. When they reached the village, they made their way through the silent streets until they came to the small railway station, and there, sitting in all her glory on a sort of small stage with two pieces of rail for her to perch on, was Madame Hortense, looking more like a very large toy than a real engine.

"Yes, that's her," said Parrot. "Looks as though she's put on a bit of rust since I last saw her. Or, maybe, it's just the moonlight."

"I'm sure she hasn't," said Penelope. "She was beautifully oiled and looked after when I saw her; she was in a wonderful state of preservation."

"Well," said Parrot, "I'll go and wake the old girl up."

So saying, he flew ahead of the children and landed on one of Madame Hortense's bumpers.

"Alors, Hortense, my little cabbage, come along," cried Parrot. "Open those big eyes of yours and let's be off."

Woken as she was out of a deep sleep, Madame Hortense uttered a short, sharp scream, which made Parrot almost fall off the bumper with astonishment.

"'Elp! 'Elp!" shouted Madame Hortense. "My assassins is 'ere again."

"Here," said Parrot, "give over. You'll have the whole village awake."

"Mon Dieu, oh it's *you*," said Madame in a husky voice with a strong French accent. "Mon Dieu, 'ow you 'ave frightened zee life from me, creeping about like zat in zee night."

34

"Who did you think it was?" asked Parrot. "Stephenson's Rocket come to pay you a visit?"

"Ah, mon Perroquet," said Madame Hortense, "always you joke. You know perfectly well zat a good-looking engine in such perfect condition as me attracts a lot of attention, n'est-ce pas? Only zee ozer night l.'ad to call for 'elp. Zere were two men from the Science Museum in London, trying to – 'ow you zay? – kidnapping me. So J 'ootled and 'ootled, and the villagers saved me. I tell you, a train of my sort does not give up easily. I am not one of zese stupid diesels."

"Of course not," said Parrot. "Why, you are without doubt the prettiest little train I've ever seen, *and* I've been around quite a bit you know."

"Ah Perroquet," sighed Madame Hortense, "you always zay zee right zing to a lady, you're so gallant, so sympathetique, mon brave Perroquet."

"Here," said Parrot. "Let me introduce my friends: Peter, Simon and Penelope."

Madame Hortense surveyed them.

"Zee boys are 'andsome," she said at last, "especially zee dark one; 'e reminds me of zee first driver I 'ad. But zee girl? . . . hm, very dull, and what a lot of rust on its head, poor zing."

"That's my hair, and it's supposed to be that colour," said Penelope, indignantly.

"Now, now, we didn't come here to start a beauty contest," said Parrot, soothingly. "We came here to ask you a favour, Hortense, my darling."

"For you, mon brave Perroquet, I will be anyzing," said Madame Hortense.

"Good," said Parrot. "Drive us to Mythologia, then."

"What?" screeched Madame Hortense. "Get out of my nice, warm siding and go up zee valley. *Me*, 'oo's retired? Me? at my age getting up zee steam. Non! non! non! nevaire! I zay, zut alors, zis you cannot ask."

The argument went on for a long time, and Parrot flattered and wheedled the little train, and the children, in turn, told her how beautiful she was, how brave she was, and how important to Mythologia she was – which was quite true.

"Well," said Madame Hortense at last, "I would do zis zing, but I cannot get down from zis comfortable rail-siding built special for me."

"Oh, that's easy," said Peter. "Two planks of wood and with your agility and skill we'll have you down in a jiffy."

"Mon Dieu, 'e flatters like you, Perroquet," said Madame Hortense. "Ah well, if it is zee fate, it is zee fate. Bring your pieces of wood and let us commence."

Quickly the two boys got some planks of wood and made a sort of slide down from the rails, on which Madame Hortense stood, to the ground below. Then they all got behind her and started to push. "Sacré couchette!" cried Madame Hortense. "'Arder, 'arder, you must propel. Alors, once again."

At last her small wheels got a purchase, and, creaking and gasping, she slid down the wooden ramp and squatted, panting, at the bottom.

"Wonderful," said Peter. "Now only a few more yards, Madame, and you'll be on the nice, comfortable railway lines."

"Zut, alors," said Madame Hortense in between gasps. "Zee zings I do for zat Perroquet."

While Peter and Simon coaxed Madame Hortense on to the lines, Penelope and Parrot searched the sidings for fuel that would make the little engine function. There was no coal, but they eventually found a pile of olive wood logs and collected armfuls of these, putting them into Madame Hortense's coal-bunker.

"Careful, careful, do not bump zee paintwork,"

panted Madame Hortense. "She was only painted nearly afresh zee ozer day."

At last the bunker was full enough of wood and they had filled up Madame Hortense's boiler from the station's tap and were ready to start. It was only when the children went aboard that they realised how tiny Madame Hortense really was, for, once Parrot and his cage were put into the engine's cab, there was only just enough room left over for the three children to squeeze in with their belongings.

"Are you aboard?" asked Madame Hortense. "Zen, will you, Peter, have zee goodness to light wiz a light my boiler?"

"It will be a pleasure, Madame," said Peter. Indeed, both he and Simon were railway enthusiasts, and so to be allowed to travel in Madame Hortense alone would have been a thrill. To be allowed to drive her was an honour. Carefully, they lit a piece of paper and then piled chips of olive wood and shreds of bark over it, coaxing it into a core of fire. Then they piled on the olive logs and soon the fire was roaring away in the furnace.

"Ah, nom de wagon-lit!" said Madame Hortense, drawing in great lungfuls of smoke and blowing them through her funnel. "Zere eez nozzing like a good smoke when one's nerves is all entanglement." Presently they got the boiler hot and soon Madame Hortense uttered the triumphant . . . "Whoosh Sh Sh Sh sssss."

"Excellent," said Parrot, admiringly. "You're in excellent voice, my dear Hortense."

"Flatterer," said Madame Hortense. "Whooshshshsh. "

"Now, Peter," said Parrot, "just ease off the brake there a bit, and, Simon, you give Madame a little more steam."

Very slowly at first, then with ever increasing speed, the wheels started to turn.

"More of zee *chuff-chuff*, *chuff-chuff*, *chuff-chuff*, steam," cried Madame Hortense. "Remove *chuff-chuff*, *chuff*, *chuff-a-*

chuff chuff chuff chuff, zee brake *chuff-chuff*, more of zee steam *chuff-a-chuff chuff-a-chuff*, *chuff-a-chuff*, *chuff-a-chuff chuff*. Alors, mes braves, we 'ave started. 'Vive La France'. *Chuff-a-chuffa chuffa, chuffa-chuffa chuffa, chuffa-chuffa chuffa . . .*"

"Wonderful," shouted Simon. "Vive Madame Hortense."

"Hear, hear," shouted Parrot.

"Have you taken your pill?" yelled Dulcibelle to Parrot. "You know you're always train-sick."

The little train gathered speed, clanking, rattling and clinking along the rails, enveloped in clouds of steam, her boiler glowing like a ruby, as Peter and Simon plied it with fresh olive wood logs, heading towards the range of mountains that lay purple and black in the moonlight.

The ride up into the valley was tremendously exciting, for the tiny railway wound to and fro in and out of the towering cliffs of rock, and ran over deep gorges where great, white waterfalls glinted in the moonlight, and where the river was pushed between jagged rocks so that it looked like the giant, glistening talons of some strange bird. Under the dark cliffs they could see the green lights of the fireflies, and above the roar of the many waterfalls and the clack and chuff of Madame Hortense's progress they could hear the plaintive "toink, toink" of the Scops owls, calling in the trees.

"We are starting up zee 'ill, *chuff-a-chuff*, *chuff-a-chuff*, *chuff-a-chuff*," panted Madame Hortense. "Make more zee steam." So Peter and Simon piled more and more logs on, and the fire grew brighter and the sparks flew out, so that the little train left a trail like a comet behind it as it chuffed on.

"Ha! ha!" laughed Parrot, as Madame Hortense went faster and faster, her little wheels singing on the rails. "By jove, you're game, Hortense my dear. Always did enjoy train travel, but with you it's positively celestial."

"Flatterer," panted Madame Hortense and gave a

couple of shrill "Wheep, wheeps" on her whistle, to show how pleased she was.

When they were half-way up the mountainside she came to a panting, gasping halt in a cloud of steam.

"Sacré Couchette," she gasped, the steam rising round her like a silver cloud in the moonlight. " 'Ere we rest for a moment and you may give me a drink."

So Peter and Simon took it in turn to fetch the water from a nearby waterfall for Madame Hortense.

Presently, with her boiler full, Madame Hortense was ready to proceed.

"It's not far now, is it, Hortense?" asked Parrot, as they climbed aboard.

"No, only a leetle bit more," she replied, as she started to chuff her way up the slope.

Soon the track levelled out, and on either side lay a deep gorge in which the river squeezed between the rocks and frothed and bubbled and winked in the moonlight. Then ahead of them stretched a cliff-face and in it were two tunnels, like two black, gaping mouths. The track at this point divided and disappeared into these two tunnels.

Madame Hortense drew to a halt by the point switch. "Pleeze to descend and switch zee points," she panted. "It eez zee left-'and tunnel we want."

Peter and Simon got down on to the track, and to-gether – for the points-lever was very stiff – they switched the points. Then they climbed aboard again.

Slowly Madame Hortense moved forward and went clackety-clack over the points and then picked up speed.

The tunnel loomed closer and closer, larger and larger, like the mouth of a yawning giant; and Penelope – not that she was frightened, but because it seemed the thing to do in the circumstances – took hold of Peter's and Simon's hands. Then "whoosh", they dived into the tunnel, and Madame Hortense startled them all by letting out two ear-splitting screams on her whistle.

"Here," shouted Parrot, "what's that for?"

"Zee bats," panted Madame Hortense. "Zay hang on zee roof, poor zings, and become suffocated if I do not warn zem."

It was very eerie going through the tunnel, because the only light they had was the light from Madame Hortense's boiler, and so they could catch only vague glimpses of the roof with its stalactites hanging down like spear-tips, dripping water.

Presently Madame Hortense gave another sharp scream on her whistle. "Pleeze to put on zee brakes, slowly," she cried. "We 'ave arrived." Slowly, Peter and Simon applied the brakes, and with much hoarse gasping and puffing the little train drew to a halt.

"All alight for Mythologia. Mythologia this stop," shouted Parrot and his voice echoed and re-echoed in the tunnel.

"A nasty, damp place," said Dulcibelle's voice. "You should be wearing your cloak. If you catch a chill, don't blame *me*."

They got down on to the track and unloaded their supplies and Parrot's cage. Then they clustered round Madame Hortense to say good-bye.

"I think you're the most wonderful train," said Penelope, "and it was a gorgeous ride. Thank you very much."

"It was nozzing, chérie," said Madame Hortense. "It doz show you what we old ones can do, n'est-ce pas?"

"Madame Hortense, it was an honour to ride in you," said Peter.

"A *privilege* and an honour, Madame," said Simon.

"You drove me very well," said Madame Hortense, "very well indeed."

"Hortense," said Parrot, "I, my friends and the whole of Mythologia are deeply grateful to you. We will never forget you."

"Dear Perroquet," said Madame Hortense, "you know, zat for you I will always do anyzing."

"You'll be all right going back?" asked Parrot.

"Yes, mon brave, I will – 'ow you say? – coast back. It eez down zee 'ill all zee way. Now, you know zee way? It eez zee branch tunnel on zee left, about fifteen metres away."

"Right," said Parrot. "We'll be off then. Goodbye, dear Hortense, and thank you again."

"Goodbye, mon Perroquet, and bon chance," sighed Madame Hortense in a sentimental cloud of steam.

Lighting their torches, the children made their way down the tunnel for about a hundred and fifty feet.

"Here it is," Parrot said suddenly. "The entrance to Mythologia." Shining their torches, the children could see a cleft in the rock on the side of the tunnel – a cleft some three feet wide and six feet high that looked rather like a narrow church door.

"This is the frontier post," explained Parrot. "Five minutes' walk and we'll be in Mythologia."

The tunnel was narrow, so that they had to go in single file. Peter went first with the torch, carrying Parrot's cage. Next came Penelope (with Parrot perched on her shoulder) carrying the food supplies, first-aid and the weapons. Then Simon brought up the rear, carrying the dinghy.

"Go a bit cautiously," whispered Parrot hoarsely. "I don't think it's very likely – because they're such slovenly creatures – but it is just possible that they may have put a sentry on duty here, to make sure I don't get back."

They rounded a corner in the passage, and Peter stopped so suddenly that Penelope bumped into him and Simon bumped into Penelope.

"What's the matter?" asked Penelope.

"Shh . . . sh," whispered Peter. "There's a light up ahead."

"Let me have a look," said Parrot, hopping off Penelope's shoulder and on to Peter's.

They stood silent, holding their breath, while Parrot peered ahead. "No, that's all right, it's not a light. It's the entrance," he said, at last. "That's the dawn you can see."

"Dawn?" said Peter. "Are you sure, Parrot? After all, it's only just half past one. It's far too early for dawn yet."

"Not in Mythologia," said Parrot. "It's dawn all day long, except when it's night."

"What on earth do you mean: 'It's dawn all day'?" asked Penelope.

"Well," explained Parrot. "When H.H. was studying to be a magician he used to have to get up at dawn, and he very soon found that it was the loveliest time of the day – all fresh and calm and the colours and everything so bright after a good night's sleep. So, when he was inventing Mythologia, he decided it would be dawn all day, except for eight hours of night. "You'll see what I mean in a minute."

Eventually, they stepped out at the end of the tunnel and stood blinking at the scene that lay before them. The sky (or what appeared to be the sky) above them, was a delicate shade of jade-green fading into pale powder-blue in places. Floating in it were armadas of tiny, fat comfortable-looking clouds, in primrose yellow, pale pink and white. The sun (or what appeared to be the sun) was just above the horizon, stationary, casting a lovely, delicate web of golden light over everything. Nearby a tiny stream – the colour of pale sherry – fell in a series of delicate waterfalls over terracotta-red rocks; and at the base of each waterfall was a deep, calm pool full of lazily-moving blue fish with scarlet fins and tails. The grass that the children stood on was deep purple, like heather, and very soft and springy to walk on; and it looked as if it had been newly mown. It was studded with innumerable, multi-coloured flowers whose petals looked as though they were made out of glass, and interspersed among them were groups of bright lemon-yellow mushrooms decorated with black spots. Farther down the valley stretched a forest of trees with big blue leaves and chocolate-coloured trunks – trunks that looked very knobbly and lumpy from a distance. Far, far on the horizon, almost hidden by morning mists, the children could see what they took to be the great inland sea which Parrot had described, gleaming and glittering like champagne in the dawn light.

"Why, it's *beautiful*," exclaimed Penelope, drawing a deep breath. "I'd never imagined it would be anything like this."

"Look at the colours," said Simon. "Aren't they *fabulous*?"

"And the sky," said Peter. "Those clouds look as though they'd been arranged."

"They are," said Parrot, "and re-arranged five times a day, so that we don't get bored. We also have four different sunsets: one, as it were, at each corner, so that those who like their sunsets red can watch one side, while those that like theirs lemon or yellow or green can watch the other sides. It's very convenient."

"I think it's *beautiful*," said Penelope. "No wonder you're proud of it."

"Well, well," said Parrot, embarrassed. "I've lived here a long time, you know. One grows fond of a place. That's why I don't want to see these darned Cockatrices take over."

"Quite right," said Peter, "and the sooner we get cracking on *that* the better. What do we do now, Parrot?"

"Well," he said judiciously, "if we follow this stream down, it joins the main river, and there we can launch the boat. Then, if my memory serves me right – and I could kick myself for not having brought a map – we travel down the main river, through Phoenix Valley, until we reach the Moon-calf Hills and Unicorn Meadows. There we're just below the Crystal Caves, and it's only a fairly short walk. However, I must warn you there are two rather nasty rapids in Phoenix Valley, and I don't see how we can avoid them. I do hope you know how to handle that dinghy of yours?"

"We'll be all right," said Peter, airily.

"Let's *hope* we'll be all right," said Simon. "With both of us paddling we should be able to manage to get through."

"Well, off we go," said Parrot. "Let's keep as much to the trees as possible, just in case there are any Cockatrices about. And remember, if you see one, they can shoot out flames to a distance of about eight feet."

"Eight feet!" exclaimed Penelope. "Good heavens, that's like a flame-thrower."

"Exactly," said Parrot. "In the old days, of course, they used to be able to kill with their glance, too, but we put a stop to that when we created Mythologia, because – really – 'enough is enough' H.H. said. It was bad enough having them going round, burning up everything they came in contact with by careless breathing, without having them kill everything with their glance as well."

"I don't know why you allowed them to come to Mythologia," said Penelope. "What do you want with a lot of horrible creatures like that?"

"Ah, no, you can't pick and choose," said Parrot. "Although certain of us, like myself, were allowed, we created Mythologia for mythical animals, and we couldn't show any favouritism. All we could do was to control their numbers, of course, which helped, and keep them in places where they did as little harm as possible. It's just unfortunate that the Cockatrices have got a bit above themselves. Anyway, with your help I'm hoping that we're going to put a stop to that."

As they were talking, they'd been walking down the

valley, following the little waterfalls and the tiny stream, and now they reached the first scattering of trees at the edge of the wood. The children looked at them in amazement.

"Ah," said Parrot. "Surprised, eh? Thought you might be. They're cork trees. Now, in the outside world, the whole business of obtaining cork is very prehistoric – if I may be allowed to criticise. First of all, you have to peel the bark off the tree and then you have to cut it into corks. Oh, it's a very laborious process. So, when we came here, H.H., among any number of spells he was using at that time, decided he'd create cork trees that saved a certain amount of time and energy. Here, as you can see, the corks grow directly on the bark of the tree, and in different sizes."

Looking round them, the children could see that Parrot was perfectly correct. On the trunk and on the branches of each tree grew corks in numerous shapes and sizes: there were tiny corks such as one would use for very small medicine bottles; there were champagne corks, wine bottle corks and great, big, flat, fat corks such as you'd use for corking up jars of preserved fruit or jam, or perhaps honey.

"Saves a lot of time, I can tell you," said Parrot. "As soon as you've made your jam, or whatever it happens to be, you just come out into one of these cork-tree forests and cut yourself off enough corks of the right shape and size. They grow again almost immediately, too, so you have an endless crop. It's rather like the grass, that grows again as soon as it's eaten by the Unicorns or Moon-calves, and it never grows any longer than it is. Anyway a nice, comfortable length, not long enough to get all damp and catch round your ankles. And the flowers too, they're one of H.H.'s inventions. A very, very inventive magician he is, I can tell you. Here, you just pluck some, and you'll see what I mean."

Penelope bent down and gathered a small bunch of the beautiful, multi-coloured flowers.

"Smell them," said Parrot.

Penelope put them up to her nose, and thought that she'd never ever in her life smelt a smell so sweet and delicious as the scent of these little flowers.

"Everlasting," said Parrot. "Stick 'em on your dressing table and they'd be there for ever, and they'll smell for ever, too; but, if you get bored with them, just throw them away. Go on, just throw them down anywhere."

Penelope threw the flowers on to the purple grass and, immediately, each one stood upright, grew little, tiny, thread-like roots which delved down into the earth, and there, lo and behold, where there'd been a scattered bunch of flowers was a little growing patch of them.

"Waste not, want not," said Parrot, winking one eye. "It's the same with the trees. If you want to light a fire, you just cut off a couple of branches of any tree that happens to be handy, and the branch grows again almost immediately. It saves the tree having that awful amputated look that trees have in the outside world. That's why everything looks so new and fresh."

Presently the stream they were following led them through the cork forest and out on to the banks of the main river.

The river was quite broad and slow-moving, and its golden waters were so transparent that, standing on the bank and looking down, the children could see porcelain white and green crabs walking about on the bottom, together with scarlet, black and yellow striped water beetles, swimming to and fro, all busy about their business.

"Is this where we set out?" said Peter.

"Yes," said Parrot. "It's about three miles from here to Phoenix Valley and then about another five miles before we reach the Moon-calf Hills."

Simon put down the dinghy and spread it out, and he and Peter and Penelope took it in turns to pump it up. At length it was ready and they launched it on to the golden waters, put Parrot's cage and all their supplies into it, and then scrambled on board and pushed off. Of all the scenes that Penelope later was to remember of Mythologia, probably the one that lived most vividly in her memory was that first trip down the river towards Phoenix Valley. The banks with their purple grass bestrewn with multi-coloured blossoms; the strange, misshapen cork-trees, their upper branches trailing long wisps of grey-green luminous moss and great fronds of what appeared to be coral-pink and green orchids. The soft sound of the water and, peering over the side, the long trailing fronds of yellow water-weed and the crabs and the busy beetles she could see beneath the boat. It was a magical experience.

Presently, however, the cork-tree forest thinned and finally disappeared, and they entered a new type of country which was barren, with the terracotta-red rocks that the children had noticed before, and in the cracks and crevices of the rocks strange cacti grew of the most weird shapes and colours.

"Not far now," said Parrot, "and we come to Phoenix Valley. I wish we had some sort of covering."

"Covering?" said Penelope. "What do you mean, covering? What would we need covering for?"

"Well, the Phoenix themselves are harmless enough," said Parrot, "but it's all those ashes flying about."

"Ashes?" said Peter. "Don't tell me there's something else that makes fire, like the Cockatrices?"

"No, no, no," said Parrot. "No, nothing like that. No, it's the Phoenix, poor dears. As you know, the Phoenix lives for about five hundred years and then it goes and sits on its nest which immediately bursts into flame and burns it up, and out of the ashes a new Phoenix is created.

As they're sensible enough to control their numbers in this way, H.H. thought the simplest thing to do – to avoid forest fires resulting in inconvenience – would be to give them a breeding valley of their own, and this is the valley we'll have to go through. It's quite a colourful spectacle really, but as I said there's a lot of ash and cinders flying about. We'll have to look a bit sharp."

As the river wound its way onwards, and Peter and Simon paddled the dinghy at a slow but steady pace, the rocky banks grew steadily higher and higher, and the stream grew swifter and swifter.

"Not far now," said Parrot. "Not far now. By the way, you haven't got a scarf or something, have you?"

"Scarf, yes," said Penelope. "I have."

"Well, tie it over your hair," said Parrot. "Just in case. Don't want to get that pretty hair burnt, do we?"

So suddenly that they were scarcely prepared for it, the river grew narrower and faster and faster, and the cliffs grew higher and higher.

"Rapids ahead," shouted Parrot.

Sure enough, red rocks stuck up like fangs and the golden waters gushed and frothed and bubbled around them. Peter and Simon were hard-pressed to manoeuvre the dinghy through without getting it holed, but they managed it and soon came into a calm stretch of river again, which had widened out between the tall cliffs.

"Whew!" said Peter, wiping his forehead. "I didn't think we were going to make that."

"Thank goodness it's over," said Simon.

"Over?" said Parrot. "That's just the first set of rapids. There's another set farther down, once we get through the valley."

Now the dinghy rounded a corner and swept into Phoenix Valley, and the sight that met their eyes was so incredible that Simon and Peter stopped paddling and sat there with their mouths open, as did Penelope, watching the strange sight that greeted their eyes on both sides of the river.

On either bank, dotted about through the valley, sat the Phoenix, like huge, multi-coloured, glittering eagles, with their wings spread out, in the way that cormorants do when they sit on the rocks to dry. Round the base of each bird there flickered and winked the fire of its nest. Periodically, one of these nests would erupt like a volcano. Great streamers of orange-red, blue and yellow flames would envelop the bird that sat there, burning it and turning it immediately into ash. So it would sit there, like a great model of its former self, made out of grey and white ash. The fire would die down and then gradually the Phoenix would start to crumble: first a few feathers from its wing, then perhaps the whole ash bird, with a sound like a great, soft sigh would crumble and fall into the fiery nest. There would be a moment's pause and then immediately the flames would start licking up again, and in their depths they could see struggling a small, multi-coloured Phoenix baby thrashing its wings and wriggling to and fro until eventually it fought its way free of the flames and zoomed up into the air, to fly gaily and happily hither and thither over the valley, like a swallow, together with all the hundreds of other Phoenix. But as Parrot had said there was a certain amount of danger, for as each Phoenix turned to ash, crumbled and fell into its nest, sparks and burning ashes flew in all directions and fell hissing into the river around them.

"Why, it's beautiful, Parrot," cried Penelope, watching the baby Phoenix struggle out of their burning nests and then fly to and fro, glittering and beautiful, across the length of the valley.

"I've never seen anything like it," said Peter. "You mean to say that each time one of those big ones turns to ash and falls into the nest it creates another one?"

"Well, it's really the same bird," said Parrot. "It's what they call a metamorphosis. That's why H.H. gave them this valley. You see, their numbers don't increase. They live for five hundred years and then they burn themselves up, like that, and are recreated again. They create a very pretty effect and they do no harm at all in Mythologia. They feed mainly on nectar, and they're very decorative."

Even though they kept the dinghy in the middle of the stream, they could still feel the heat of the burning Phoenix' nests on either bank. It took them, perhaps, half an hour to work their way through the nesting sites, and then gradually the river started to narrow again.

"Now," said Parrot, worriedly, "this is the difficult part. We've got one set of rapids before we reach calm water. If we can get through this, we're all right."

"Is everything lashed down, Penny?" asked Simon.

"Yes," she said, "everything. I don't know about the stuff inside Parrot's cage."

"Oh, that'll be all right," said Parrot. "I've had that secured for ages."

As they were talking, the dinghy had started to drift closer and closer towards the shore, unnoticed by both Peter and Simon. Just on the edge of the bank was an enormous Phoenix nest, with the bird sitting in it with its wings outspread, already turned to ash by the flames. Suddenly, the dinghy bumped against the bank just below the nest.

"Hi," shouted Peter. "Look out."

"Push off, push off quick," said Simon, looking at the great ash bird towering above them.

But they were too late. Just at that moment the monstrous, great ash-phoenix started to crumble, and with a tremendous "Whoo . . . shsh . . ." it fell into its nest and enveloped the dinghy and its occupants in burning ash and multi-coloured sparks.

"Paddle out into mid-stream, paddle out into mid-stream," cried Simon. "Quick! Quick!"

Rapidly he and Peter paddled the dinghy out into mid-stream, but it was so full of burning ash that there was nothing they could do. Suddenly, there was a sharp plop and a hissing noise, and they could feel the dinghy shrinking under them.

"Look out," shouted Peter. "Look out."

The current caught the rapidly deflating dinghy and whirled it away down river, and then suddenly there was no dinghy under them any more. Penelope fell into the water and it closed over her head, and she was whirled away, over and over, into the darkness and roar of the second set of rapids.

three

MOON-CALVES AND UNICORNS

When Penelope regained consciousness, she found herself lying on a sandbank, with her head in Peter's lap, and Simon leaning over her anxiously, rubbing her hands, while Parrot paced up and down, muttering to himself.

"She's come to," said Simon, with obvious relief.

"Are you all right, Penny?" asked Peter anxiously.

"Speak to us, dearest Penelope," said Parrot, peering earnestly into her face, his blue eyes full of tears, his bright feathers bedraggled with river water.

They all looked so woebegone and worried that Penelope wanted to laugh, but she didn't dare.

"Of course, I'm all right," she said, sitting up and feeling rather sick and headachy. "I just feel as though I've swallowed half the river and been dragged through the rapids backwards."

"A remarkably perspicacious description, if I may say so," exclaimed Parrot. "That's exactly what did happen to you."

"Where are we?" said Penelope, looking round.

"Well, we were swept through the rapids after the boat sank," said Peter. "You were caught under the water amongst some rocks and Simon and I had to dive for you, but we got you up at last and managed to swim to the sandbank with you."

The sandbank, one of several, was a long narrow one that stretched nearly the width of the river. On it, to the children's astonished delight, had been washed all their belongings, including the now useless dinghy.

"What on earth are we going to do now that we can't use the dinghy?" said Simon.

"Everything can be set to rights when we find some Moon-calves," said Parrot, testily.

"What's all this about Moon-calves?" asked Penelope, attempting rather unsuccessfully to wring the water out of her clothes.

"I don't know," said Peter. "Parrot keeps on about them as if they were the one thing we'd come here to find."

"My dear Peter," said Parrot severely, "if I tell you that the Moon-calves are by far away one of the most important of H.H.'s inventions and that they are, without doubt, *the* most important animal, agriculturally and economically speaking, in Mythologia, then perhaps you'll comprehend why it's important for us to find some."

"No," said Peter.

"You are a singularly simple-minded boy," said Parrot sternly. "I'm now going to leave you and go in search of a Moon-calf herd. Kindly wait here for my return." So saying, Parrot stalked into his water-logged cage and opened his Louis Quinze cupboard.

"If you're going out like that, all wet, you'll catch a chill," said Dulcibelle, "and it doesn't do you any good to be flying all over the countryside at your age."

"Oh, be quiet," said Parrot crossly. "You're supposed to be my singing spider and house-keeper, not a jailer. Where did you put my telescope?"

"It's where you left it – in the cupboard, and you shouldn't speak to me like that. Here I slave away all day and what thanks do I get, eh? Tell me that. All you do is to try to drown us all and create a lot of extra work. Look at the place – drenched, carpet ruined . . . I'll have to air the bed. But do you care? Oh no! All you think about is flying round the countryside with your telescope. You should know better at your age. You carry on as if you were a fledgling."

At last from the strange collection of clothes and other things in his cupboard, Parrot managed to unearth a handsome, brass-bound telescope which he held carefully in his beak. "Reconnaissance," he explained to the children, somewhat indistinctly. "Back shortly. I should have some breakfast, if I were you." So saying, he flew off, his wings flashing rainbow colours in the sunlight.

Penelope decided that Parrot's suggestion of breakfast was a good one, for once they got on the move again there was no knowing when they would have a chance to eat. So she divided out a large bar of chocolate between herself and the boys and gave them a handful of raisins and almonds each. Surprisingly, they found they were remarkably hungry when they started to eat. Dulcibelle declined the offer of chocolate, raisins or nuts.

"You haven't, I suppose, got a grasshopper about you?" she asked wistfully, "or a couple of house-flies?"

"No, I'm sorry," said Penelope.

"Ah well, I didn't think you would," said Dulcibelle. "Never mind."

Their hunger satisfied, the children spread out their belongings on the sand to dry. They had just finished when they heard a voice crying: "Ahoy, there, ahoy," and Parrot flew into view and performed a very neat landing on the sandbank.

"Excellent news," he panted, removing the telescope from his beak and putting it under his wing. "There's a herd of Moon-calves about half a mile away. I missed them the first time – the silly things were all grazing under trees."

"So," said Peter, "what do we do now?"

"Go and get some jelly," said Parrot.

"Jelly?" asked Simon. "Did you say 'jelly'?"

"Yes," said Parrot, impatiently. "You and Peter come with me, and Penelope can stay here with Dulcibelle."

"No," said Penelope, firmly, "if you're going hunting for Moon-calves or jelly or whatever it is, I want to come too."

"Oh, all right," said Parrot. "Dulcibelle can stay here."

"No," said Dulcibelle. "What if a crocodile should come?"

"There are no crocodiles here, you know that perfectly well," said Parrot.

"You know, Dulcibelle," Penelope said hastily, "if you *did* stay here, it would make Parrot think even more highly of you."

Dulcibelle thought about it for a moment. "All right," she said at last, "I'll stay, but you're not to be more than three days, mind."

"Come on, then," said Parrot. "You'll all have to wade over to the bank. There's a shallow bit over there, and then I'll show you where the herd is."

So the children waded across from the sandbank, leaving Dulcibelle as guardian of their things, and set off over the purple grass field, dotted with flowers, towards the distant cork forest.

"What are Moon-calves?" asked Penelope of Parrot, who was perched on her shoulder.

"The most *useful* creatures," said Parrot, "but I must confess they are the result of an accident rather than design. You see it was in the early days of Mythologia when H.H. was still busy creating useful things like the cork-trees, for example. Well, he was trying to invent a cow which would give a never-ending yield of milk, but he had to use the mythological Moon-calf as a basis, so that it would fit in. It was just unfortunate that on that particular day he had lost his glasses, and in consequence he got three or four spells muddled up into one by mistake. It was all right, as it turned out. Poor H.H. was most distressed at the time. However, since then, they've proved to be most successful."

They made their way through the trees, towards where they could hear the clonking of a bell and a gentle mooing noise, like the sound of an ordinary herd of cattle in a meadow. Then they came out into a clearing, and there was the Moon-calf herd. The children looked at the creatures in amazement.

"A bit surprising at first glance, aren't they?" said Parrot proudly.

"*Surprising?* They're the weirdest things I've ever *seen*," said Peter.

"They look like bits and pieces of all sorts of things," said Penelope.

Basically, the Moon-calves were like giant, dark-green snails with extremely pretty golden and green shells perched on their backs, but, instead of having horns in front, like a snail, they had the fat head of a baby bull-calf with amber-coloured horns and a great mop of curls lying between them. They had dark, liquid eyes, and they moved slowly over the purple grass, browsing just like cows, but moving like snails. Occasionally, one of them would lift up its head and utter a long and soulful, "Moo ooo".

"Are they dangerous?" asked Simon, watching them, fascinated.

"Lordy, no," said Parrot. "The kindest, stupidest things in the whole country, but, like most kind and stupid people, exceedingly useful."

"But what does it supply?" asked Penelope.

"Milk," said Parrot, "and Moon-calf jelly, probably one of the most useful substances known."

"Where do you milk them from?" asked Peter puzzled.

"The shell," said Parrot. "Each shell's got three taps on it: two are marked 'hot' and 'cold' – just turn the tap and there you are: hot or cold milk whichever you like."

"And the third tap?" asked Simon.

"Cream," said Parrot.

"Gosh!" said Peter, who was passionately devoted to cream. "They *are* useful creatures."

"And the jelly?" asked Penelope. "What about that?"

"Ah," said Parrot. "Well, you know how a snail leaves a slimy trail behind him? Well, Moon-calves do the same, except it's Moon-calf jelly, and they only do it when asked."

"Ugh," said Penelope. "What's the use of a lot of jelly?"

"It hardens into sheets," said Parrot, "and then becomes a most useful product. For one thing it's cold when it's hot, and it's hot when it's cold."

"What?" said Peter, thoroughly confused.

"What I mean is, if you make it into a house or clothes, or something like that," said Parrot. "It's hot in cold weather and vice versa."

"That's useful," said Simon thoughtfully.

"You store it in sheets," Parrot went on, "and then just take out a sheet when you want it and think it into something."

"*Think* it into something?" said Penelope. "What on earth do you mean?"

"I'll have to show you," said Parrot. "Here, let's go closer."

They walked up to the Moon-calf herd, and the strange animals lifted their heads and gazed at them in the friendliest fashion, munching the mauve grass and uttering an occasional soft "moo". They located the leader of the herd, which was larger than the others and wore a large gold bell around its neck, marked "Leader".

"Good morning," said Parrot.

The leader gazed at them and then let out a prolonged "MOO ooo" of greeting.

"Not very good conversationalists," whispered Parrot into Penelope's ear. "Very restricted vocabulary."

The leading Moon-calf continued to gaze at them soulfully.

"Now, old girl," said Parrot. "We want a couple of sheets of jelly. Do you think you can provide them without too much strain?" The leader solemnly nodded her head. Then she turned to the herd and uttered a prolonged, quavering "MOOooo". The herd immediately formed a circle, nose to tail, and the leader took up its position in the centre. Then, when they were ready, the leader started to sing – that's to say she shook her head to and fro so that her bell clanged discordantly, and cried "MOOoooooo, MOOoooooo, MOOooooo". As she did so, the whole herd started to slide round in a circle and say very rapidly and in chorus: "Moo-moo-moo, Moo-moo-moo, Moo-moo-moo."

The resulting sound was noisy and dismal in the extreme, but the children noticed that as the herd slid round and round, every other Moon-calf left a trail of what looked like jade-green, liquid glue, and the Moon-calf behind it steam-rollered it into a thin, flat, transparent sheet.

"All right, all right, that's enough, *that's enough*," Parrot shouted, to make himself heard above the chorus of "Moos". The Moon-calves, looking somewhat surprised, came to a halt, and their mooing died away. Lying on the grass were some twenty sheets of what looked like very thin, brittle, green glass.

"They never could count," said Parrot, in exasperation. "Still, never mind, it'll come in useful."

Picking up one of the sheets, Penelope found it was as light as a cobweb and easily bent.

"Why, it's a little like a sort of plastic," she said.

"Better than plastic," said Parrot, "because as soon as

you've finished with it you just think it into oblivion, so there's none of it left around mucking up the scenery."

"What do you mean: 'think it into oblivion'?" asked Peter.

"Well, we only want two sheets," said Parrot. "So I'll get rid of the rest. Watch."

The children watched fascinated, as Parrot walked from sheet to sheet of the jelly, glared at it in intense concentration and said: "Disappear."

The sheets immediately rolled themselves up into a tube and then got smaller and smaller until, with the noise of the bursting of a very tiny balloon, they disappeared.

"Incredible," said Simon.

"I've never seen anything like it," said Peter.

"So you simply *tell* them what to do?" asked Penelope.

"Yes," said Parrot, mopping his brow with his wing. "It requires a lot of concentration, though. Then, of course, you have to think them into being anything you want, anything inanimate, that is. Watch."

He went up to one of the two remaining sheets of Moon-calf jelly and held out his wing. "Give me two pieces of you, eighteen inches by sixteen," he said, and the sheet obligingly tore off two pieces of itself exactly that size.

Parrot flew on to Penelope's shoulder. "Now," he said, "stand still while I think them into something."

The children watched with bated breath.

"What are you going to think them into?" asked Simon.

"Buckets," said Parrot, glaring at the pieces of jelly.

The children watched and they saw the jelly turn from pale green to dark green, and then it suddenly gave a wriggle, and it wriggled and writhed, twisted and jumped, curling itself into all sorts of contortions. Then it gave an extra complicated wriggle – there was a faint "pop" and there were two beautiful small buckets standing in front of them.

"I say, that's *wonderful*," said Peter, much impressed.

"No wonder you said it was so useful," observed Simon.

"It's the most useful thing I've ever *seen*," said Penelope, with conviction.

Parrot proceeded to fill one bucket with cold milk and one with cream from the shell of one of the Mooncalves. Then they thanked the herd, which said "Moo" politely and in unison, and taking the sheets of jelly made their way back to the river and their belongings.

"So *there* you are," said Dulcibelle, when they got back. "Took your time, didn't you? I was just about to send out a search party."

"How could you send out a search party? – you exaggerating, egocentric spider," asked Parrot.

"We've brought you some cream," said Penelope, hastily.

"Cream?" said Dulcibelle. "How nice. No greenfly to go with it, I suppose?"

"I'm afraid not," said Penelope, gravely.

"Oh well," said Dulcibelle. "It's to be expected, I suppose."

Then Parrot, with much concentration, thought the jelly into a splendid new dinghy and, filling it full of their equipment and Parrot's cage, they launched her on to the placid river.

"Yo ho ho, and all that sort of rot," said Parrot gaily. "Not long now and we'll come to the Unicorn Meadows. Then it's only a half hour's climb to the Crystal Caves."

"I'm longing to see the Unicorns," said Penelope, trailing her hands in the golden, glittering waters, as Peter and Simon paddled them along at a good pace.

"Very decorative animals, I must admit," said Parrot judiciously.

"Very, very standoffish, if you know what I mean, like to keep themselves to themselves. Snobs! Always saying: 'Well, it's none of our business' – when of course it is, because, after all, everything's everyone's business in Mythologia. I mean we've all got to *believe* in each other, otherwise we'll all vanish, won't we?"

"Perhaps they're just timid," suggested Penelope.

"Timid? Not them," said Parrot. "They'll take on anything. No, they're just lazy. When I went to see them about this Cockatrice business, you know what they said? It made me mad, it did. They said: 'What business is it of ours? It's up to you and H.H. to control the unruly elements among us.' Ha! I'll give them unruly elements when we get back into power."

"The forest is ending," said Peter, who was in the front of the dinghy. "It looks as though we're coming to open country."

"Just let me go and reconnoitre," said Parrot.

Taking his telescope, he flew off, and was gone a few minutes. Then he returned to the dinghy, circled it with great skill and landed on Penelope's shoulder. "All clear," he said, "couldn't see a thing. Make for that little cove up ahead and we'll land there."

They landed in the cove, deflated the dinghy and packed it up. Then they set off over the rolling meadowland, dotted with great clumps of blue bushes, covered in magenta-red flowers the size of sunflowers. About two miles away lay a range of forested hills, and it was there that the Crystal Caves lay, according to Parrot. Although the sun had not risen any higher above the horizon, it had become much warmer, and the boys found it was hot work lugging Parrot's home with all its furniture plus their supplies and the dinghy. When they got to what Parrot said was the half-way mark, he told them they could have a rest – and thankfully they put down their loads and lay down in the shade of one of the big blue bushes and had a much-needed drink of the Moon-calf milk.

"I'll just walk up to the brow of the hill and make sure it's all clear ahead," said Penelope. "You all have a good rest."

"Well, be careful," said Peter. "Don't go too far."

"Oh, it's open country round here, I don't think she'll come to much harm," said Parrot, dozing on top of his cage.

"Well, I shan't go far, anyway," said Penelope.

"Let us know what you see," said Simon lazily, half-asleep, "and if you see any Cockatrices, don't forget to run."

"Don't worry, I won't," said Penelope.

She walked slowly up the slope, enjoying the balmy air, and the beautifully coloured sky and the soft springy grass underfoot. When she reached the top of the hill, she looked down into the next valley and was admiring the colour scheme of mauve grass, blue bushes and magenta flowers, when she suddenly saw a small animal rush out of one clump of bushes and bound into the next. But it happened so quickly that she couldn't tell what sort of animal it was, so she concealed herself in one of the blue bushes and sat there quietly, waiting for it to reappear. Presently it did so, and Penelope caught her breath in surprise and delight, for it was a pale lavender-coloured baby Unicorn with huge dark-blue eyes. Its mane and tail were like spun gold and its tiny horn was like a twisted stick of transparent, golden barley sugar. The Unicorn stood, every muscle taut, its ears pricked forward, its nostrils wide, looking back the way it had come. It was obvious that something was chasing it, and the baby was not sure whether it had shaken off its pursuer or not.

Then Penelope's blood ran cold, for over the brow of the hill, strutting like an enormous coloured cockerel, came a Cockatrice. It paused and looked about it, its cruel, greeny-gold eyes glittering, its scales gleaming gold and red in the sun. As it moved its head to look around, Penelope could hear its scales rustling and clattering together, and she could see the wisps of blue smoke trailing from its nostrils and the tiny flicker of orange flames springing up and dying down as it breathed. The Unicorn must have seen it too, for it turned round and bounded along the valley, dodging in and out of the blue bushes until it stopped, panting, not far from where Penelope sat concealed. She could see its nostrils widening and its ribs heaving as its breath rasped in and out. It was obvious that the Cockatrice had been pursuing it for some time.

The Cockatrice, having surveyed the valley, twitched the end of its forked tail to and fro, like a cat; then it bent its great cockerel's head forward and started sniffing the ground, uttering a low snarling noise to itself – one of the most horrible sounds Penelope had ever heard. The Unicorn, hearing this and obviously too exhausted to run any farther, crouched down and laid back its ears, its eyes wide with terror. Suddenly the Cockatrice must have picked up the scent, for it uttered a pleased, blood-curdling crow, and started down into the valley.

Penelope was in a terrible predicament. She wanted desperately to help the baby Unicorn, and yet she knew it would be dangerous for her and her companions to attract the attention of the Cockatrice. But, as she sat there, she decided on a plan of action – a dangerous plan, but one that might work. She had noticed that the Cockatrice seemed very bad at tracking by scent, for several times it lost it altogether and wandered round in circles, clucking to itself. Penelope decided that if the baby Unicorn's track was broken, the Cockatrice might well lose it altogether. There was only one way of doing that, and that was to change the Unicorn's track for one of her own. She knew her plan was horribly risky and that, if it failed, both she and the Unicorn might be burnt to death by the infuriated Cockatrice. But she knew that if she thought about it – and the risks involved – for too long, her courage might fail her, so she got to her feet and ran down into the valley, zigzagging through the bushes to where the Unicorn lay, and then she gathered it up into her arms. The Unicorn, obviously thinking that it was being attacked from behind by another Cockatrice, gave a tiny whinny of terror and started to kick and butt her with its horn.

"Stop struggling, you silly thing," hissed Penelope. "Stop struggling. I'm a friend. I'm trying to help you."

At the word "friend" the Unicorn stopped struggling and lay in her arms, looking up into her face with its big terrified eyes as dark-blue as pansies.

"Friend?" it asked in a soft voice. "Friend?"

"Yes," whispered Penelope. "Now lie quiet and I'll try to save you."

In spite of the fact that the Unicorn was as small as a fox terrier, it was quite a weight as Penelope soon discovered. She ran back up the hillside, dodging from bush to bush, only moving when the Cockatrice had its head down to smell the ground, for she was not sure how keen its eyesight was. Panting, she reached the top of the slope and then watched to see if her trick would succeed. What would happen if the Cockatrice started to follow her trail, she dreaded to think, nor had she any idea what she would do if this happened. The Cockatrice was now nearing the spot where Penelope had picked up the baby Unicorn, and she watched it, holding her breath. Suddenly, the Cockatrice, which had its beak to the ground, sniffing to and fro, reared up with a startled snarl. Its eyes closed and it sneezed suddenly and violently. Flames and smoke shot from its nostrils and burnt a great, black patch on the purple grass. It sneezed again and again uncontrollably, and each time it did so it burnt a great patch of grass or set fire to a bush. To Penelope's amazement it didn't seem able to stop, it was behaving like someone with hay-fever. At last, its eyes watering and still sneezing violently, it turned and ran off, leaving a trail of blackened grass and smouldering bushes behind it.

"Well," said Penelope, not knowing whether to be amused or annoyed. "I didn't know I smelt that bad. Anyway, at least it's gone."

"Thank you for saving me," said the baby Unicorn in its soft voice. "It was very kind and very brave of you."

"Well, I don't know about that," said Penelope. "It was successful, which was the main thing, but what on earth were you doing, being chased by a Cockatrice? What were you doing out alone? Where are your father and mother?"

"The herd's over there," said the Unicorn. "I slipped away from it because I wanted to go and practise my butting."

"Your what?" asked Penelope.

"Butting," said the Unicorn, nodding his head up and down, so that his horn glittered. "You know, with my horn. We have the Great Butting Contest every year, and this year I'm old enough to enter for it, and being Crown Prince I've got to win, you see."

"Crown Prince?" asked Penelope, wondering if she had heard aright.

"Yes," said the baby. "I'm Septimus, Crown Prince of the Unicorns. My mother and father are the king and queen."

"All the more reason why you shouldn't be running around on your own," said Penelope, severely. "Think — Crown Prince of the Unicorns being beaten by a Cockatrice."

"I know," said Septimus, contritely, "but I *had* to

65

practise my butting and the cork forests are the best place for that, because it doesn't hurt your horn so much if you choose a big cork."

"Do your mother and father know that you were going there?" asked Penelope.

"No," said Septimus. "They always make such a *fuss*."

"Well, they must be worried to death," said Penelope. "The sooner we get you back to them, the better."

"Yes," said Septimus, "but, please, will you explain to them that it wasn't my fault that I was chased by a Cockatrice?"

"All right," said Penelope. "Why did the Cockatrice chase you?"

"He said he wanted to take me to their castle, so that the Cockatrices would have control over the Unicorns," said Septimus. "And he caught me once, but I gave him a jolly good butt and got away. He didn't dare use his fire, because he wanted me alive, you see. I'm glad he didn't, because he might have singed my mane and tail, and they're rather beautiful, aren't they?"

Penelope shivered. "Yes, very. Well, you'd better come with me to my friends and we'll see about getting you back to your family."

So they went back to join the others, Septimus gambolling gaily around Penelope, apparently having quite forgotten his recent narrow escape. When they reached the others, Peter and Simon were enchanted to meet a real, live Unicorn for the first time, but horrified at the risk Penelope had taken to save it from the Cockatrice. "Honestly, I *would* have called you all, if I could have," she protested, "but I had no time. I had to act at once."

"I hope this idiotic creature is grateful to you," said Parrot severely. "He doesn't deserve to be saved, playing truant like that." But Septimus wasn't listening. He'd found a small puddle under some bushes and was gazing entranced at his own reflection.

"They're all the same, these Unicorns," said Parrot gloomily. "Vain as vain. Give them a mirror, or, in fact, anything they can see their reflection in and they carry on as though they're hypnotised."

"Well, he's only a baby," said Penelope, "and he *is* rather beautiful, you must admit."

"They're *all* like that," said Parrot, "especially his mother and father. Well, I suppose we'd better be getting on our way and return him to the bosom of his family.'

So they set off once again, with Septimus prancing to and fro around them.

"Do you think I look better with my horn like *thi*. or . . . like *this*, Penelope?" he asked for the hundredth time.

"If you don't be quiet," said Parrot, irritably, "I shall borrow Penelope's scissors and cut off your mane and tail."

This dire threat had the desired effect on Septimus and he became very subdued and even asked Penelop whether he could carry something for her.

As they were making their way through a clearing in the great, blue, bushes, there was a sudden rumbling noise like thunder, and the earth shook beneath their feet. Before they had a chance to do anything sensible, a host of lavender and white Unicorns came crashing through the bushes, their hooves thrumming on the turf, and came to a snorting halt a few feet away from the party, so that the children found themselves encircled by a hedge of sharp, golden horns, all pointing at them menacingly.

"Hey up!" shouted Parrot. "Hey up! No need for all that nonsense – it's only *us*."

The solid circle of Unicorns parted and through their ranks came a very large Unicorn of the deep and beautiful lavender colour. His mane and tail were pale honey-amber and his twisted horn glittered like newly-minted golden sovereigns. It was obvious that this was the King of the Unicorns and obvious also that the slender white Unicorn with the golden mane and tail, that followed him, was the Queen.

"Why, Parrot, it's *you*," said the King in surprise.

"Of course, it's me, who did you expect?" asked Parrot.

"We were told that since the Cockatrices had taken over, you had fled the country," said the Unicorn.

"What?" said Parrot, indignantly. "*Me?* flee the country, *me?*"

"Well, we thought it was unlike you," said the Unicorn, "but even H.H. said you'd disappeared without even leaving a note, and the Cockatrices said you had fled."

"I'll give them '*fled*' when I get back," said Parrot grimly.

"Yes," said Peter. "Fled indeed. We'll show them, don't you worry, Parrot."

"It'll be the Cockatrices that will be doing the fleeing, when we've finished with them," said Simon. "Why they're so stupid that one of them was fooled even by my cousin here."

"Hey," said Penelope protestingly. "What do you mean 'even by your cousin'."

"I didn't mean it the way it sounded," said Simon hastily. "What I meant was that it does show the Cockatrices are stupid and can be fooled."

"Penelope saved me from a Cockatrice," said Septimus, and went on to tell his father and mother (with a certain amount of exaggeration) how Penelope had fooled the Cockatrice.

"The whole of the Unicorn herd is in your debt," said the King, his eyes flashing. "From now on every Unicorn in Mythologia is your servant. You've only to make a request and we'll do our best to grant your wish. In the meantime, I'll put four of my subjects at your disposal –

one for each of you to ride, one to carry Parrot and your belongings."

"I'm most grateful to your Majesty," said Penelope. "It's very generous of you. I wonder if I could make a small request?"

"Speak," said the Unicorn. "If it lies within my power, your wish will be granted."

"Then, will you and your subjects join forces with Parrot, my cousins and myself in our efforts to overthrow these ill-mannered and dangerous Cockatrices?" she asked.

"We Unicorns generally keep ourselves to ourselves," said the King. "We do not meddle in other people's affairs. But, as this is your wish, and as a Cockatrice had the audacity to try to steal my son, I hereby declare that all the Unicorns in Mythologia, including myself, will serve under you until such time as the Cockatrices are vanquished."

"Thank you," said Penelope. "Thank you *very* much."

"Dendrological dandelions!" exclaimed Parrot. "That's the stuff. Together we can defeat and destroy those truly flamboyant, futile and filibustering Cockatrices."

So the children piled their belongings and Parrot's cage on to the broad back of one Unicorn and climbed on to the backs of three others.

"Remember," said the King, "when you want us, send us a message and we will come instantly. There are a hundred and fifty sharp horns at your disposal."

"Thank you, your Majesty," said Penelope.

"We'll be in touch as soon as we've worked out a plan of campaign with H.H." said Parrot. "Now, be a good chap and tell your people not to breathe a word about having seen us, will you? Surprise is half the battle, you know."

"None of my subjects will say anything," the King assured him.

"Well, we'll be off then," said Parrot, climbing on to Penelope's shoulder. "Sooner we get to the Crystal Caves the better."

So the little cavalcade of Unicorns, carrying the children and their belongings, set off towards the forested hills that lay about half a mile away.

"That was clever of you to enlist the aid of the Unicorns," Parrot whispered in Penelope's ear. "Quick thinking."

"But it seems so silly that they shouldn't join us," Penelope whispered back. "After all, Mythologia is as much their country as yours, so why shouldn't they help?"

"Quite right," said Parrot. "Quite right. Even with their help, it's going to be a struggle to defeat the Cockatrices. They must be *very* sure of their position to risk annoying the Unicorns by trying to take Septimus."

"Well, aren't there other creatures in Mythologia whose help we can get?" asked Peter, riding alongside Penelope, while Simon rode on her left.

"Well, yes," said Parrot, "but none of them is a lot of use. I mean, the Moon-calves, for example. Useful creatures but not cut out for this sort of thing. The Griffons will probably join us – that would be a help. The Dragons *would* have been of some help to us if Tabitha hadn't behaved so stupidly."

"Yes, what actually did Tabitha do?" asked Simon.

"I'll tell you when we get there," said Parrot. "It's just through these trees."

They wound their way through a thicket of cork-trees, and there ahead stretched a high terracotta-red cliff and they could see the arched entrance to a cave in it. As they came nearer they could see that all the grass round the cave entrance was charred and the bushes blackened and burnt.

"It's those Cockatrices again," exploded Parrot angrily.

"They've been up here trying to get at H.H. Just look how they've burnt the undergrowth."

"I hope they haven't hurt Mr Junketberry," Penelope said, remembering, with a shiver, the way the Cockatrice had snarled when it was chasing Septimus.

"Shouldn't think so," said Parrot. "The Crystal Caves are a special design. If you're outside, you can't get in, and if you're inside, you can't get out."

Like everything else in Mythologia this sounded highly confusing, and the children said so.

"Well," said Parrot, 'when we discovered the Caves, they were just ordinary caves, but H.H. invented a sort of liquid crystal that could be produced like foam, and then it would harden. He was so proud of it that he filled the caves with it. The result is that once you get inside it's like walking through giant soap bubbles. It's transparent so that you can see in any direction, but it's jolly difficult to get there, unless you know your way about. It's like being in a transparent maze. H.H. and I are the only ones that really know how to get in and out."

By now they had dismounted at the mouth of the huge cave and the children could see that it did, in fact, look as if the cave was full of huge soap bubbles, transparent and delicate, with a rainbow tinge to them, just like real bubbles.

"Now," said Parrot to the Unicorns. "You chaps had better graze quietly out here until we want you again."

The Unicorns nodded their heads amiably and wandered off into the cork forest.

"Follow me," said Parrot, having delved into his cupboard and produced a compass.

And the children picked up their belongings and Parrot's cage, and followed him into the Crystal Caves. Penelope felt it was rather like walking through a transparent cloud. On every side they could see branch tunnels stretching away, it seemed for ever, yet each way they turned they were met, as in a maze, by a wall of shimmering crystal.

"Third right, second left, fifth right, fourth left," Parrot muttered to himself, as he trotted along, keeping a sharp eye on his compass.

The crystal corridors were lit by pale green light, and Simon, wondering where it came from, asked Parrot.

"Glow worms," Parrot explained. "H.H. gave them the entire roof, on condition that they lit the corridors. Of course, the main living areas are lit by mushrooms."

"Mushrooms?" asked Peter.

"Yes, luminous mushrooms – give a very good light," said Parrot.

Now they were deep in the Caves and the crystal bubbles appeared to be getting larger and larger. Presently, through the many layers of transparent crystal ahead of them, they could see a strong, white glow.

"Nearly there," muttered Parrot, "nearly there. I bet poor H.H. is at his wits' end about me. We'll soon solve the problem, now we're here."

They rounded a corner and came into a huge, oval, crystal room, lit by bunches of white, phosphorescent mushrooms hung upside down from the ceiling. It had two semi-circular alcoves leading off it. In the main room there was a long table and a number of high-back chairs in silver-coloured wood and several low comfortable couches covered with brightly coloured cushions. In one of the semi-circular alcoves was a huge kitchen range with various pots and pans bubbling on it, and above it hung what looked like hams and sausages and strings of what appeared to be onions. In the next alcove was set up a laboratory – bunsen burners, retorts, test tubes, pestles and mortars, and innumerable bottles of various coloured herbs and salts. Standing with his back to them, and holding a bow and arrow that was bigger than he, stood a short, fat figure in black and gold robes, with a gold and black pointed hat on his head.

"Avast," cried this apparition, shaking the bow and arrow in the most unprofessional way. "Avast. One more step and I'll put an arrow through your gizzard, you foul and disobedient Cockatrices."

"Oh dear," said Parrot. "He's lost his glasses again."

"Avast. One step nearer and I'll shoot to kill," said H.H., waving his bow about.

"H.H.!" shouted Parrot. "It's me, Parrot."

Hearing Parrot's voice behind him, H.H. wheeled round and his hat fell off. To the children's surprise (for they had thought, somehow, magicians were all tall and lanky, and grey like herons) H.H. had a jolly round face and a long white beard to his waist, and long white hair through which the top of his bald head peeped like a pink mushroom.

"Foul Cockatrice," cried H.H., glaring round wildly. "How dare you pretend to be Parrot. Do you think that I'd be deceived by such an impertinent imitation?"

"Oh dear," said Parrot. "I do *wish* he'd put his glasses where he could find them, or better still not take them off."

So saying, he flew down the room and landed on H.H.'s shoulder. "H.H. it's me, *really* me, Parrot. I've come back," said Parrot in H.H.'s ear.

"Parrot, Parrot, is that really *you*?" asked H.H. in a quavering voice, and he put up a fat, trembling hand to stroke Parrot's plumage.

" 'Course it is," said Parrot.

"Oh, Parrot, I am pleased you're back," said H.H.

"And I'm glad to be back," said Parrot.

"Well now, well now," said H.H. at last, blowing his nose vigorously and walking into a chair. "Where have you been, Parrot? I've been looking all over for you. I felt sure that those abominable Cockatrices had burnt you up."

"It was those Toads," said Parrot, "they leapt on us in the night, turned me and Dulcibelle into a vulgar brown paper parcel and pushed us into the river."

"The impertinence of it, the impertinence of it," said H.H., starting to pace up and down, and his face growing red with anger. He was so agitated that he walked into the crystal wall and fell down. Peter and Simon helped him to his feet.

"Thank you, thank you, too kind," murmured H.H. "Then what happened, Parrot?"

"Well," said Parrot, "we were washed up on a beach in the outside world and were found by these kind children."

"What children?" asked H.H., peering round.

"The ones standing next to you," said Parrot, patiently.

"Deary me, are those children?" asked H.H "I thought they were chairs. How do you do, children?" He waved a friendly hand to some nearby chairs.

"The sooner I find your glasses for you the better," observed Parrot. "Anyway, if it had not been for the courage and helpfulness of these children, I should not be here."

"Then I'm deeply in your debt," said H.H., trying to shake hands with a chair. "Very deeply in your debt."

"Now, before we go any further," said Parrot, "let me find your glasses. Where did you leave them? Where did you have them last?"

"I'm not altogether sure," said H.H. helplessly. "First there was this Cockatrice business, and I lost the first pair. Then I had Tabitha on my hands in a most hysterical state, I must say, and I lost the second pair; and I've forgotten where I put the spare pair that I wear when I lose the other two pairs."

"Well, stand still until I come back here," said Parrot,

"or you'll only hurt yourself." He flew off down the room and started searching in various places.

"Would you like to sit down, Mr Junketberry?" asked Penelope, laying her hand on H.H.'s arm. "There's a couch just behind you."

"Oh er . . . yes, thank you," said H.H. "But please call me H.H. Everyone does."

"Thank you," said Penelope, helping him to sit down on the couch.

"Are you a girl-child?" inquired H.H., peering up at her.

"Yes," said Penelope, smiling. "I'm Penelope and these are my cousins, Peter and Simon."

"How de do, how de do," said H.H., bobbing his head in the general direction of Peter and Simon. "I was thinking that if you're a girl-child, perhaps you could go to soothe Tabitha. You know, as one woman to another?"

"I haven't any experience in soothing Dragons," said Penelope in alarm. "I'm not at all sure that I'd be awfully good at it, you know."

"I'm sure you would," said H.H., beaming at her. "You have *such* a kind voice. How generous of you to offer. I'll take you to her as soon as I get my glasses."

At that moment Parrot swooped back with a pair of glasses in his beak. "Here," he said, giving them to H.H. "They were in the jar of Moon-carrot Jam. What were they doing there?"

"Ah, yes," said H.H. pleasedly, putting them on. "I remember putting them in there, because it was the most unlikely place to put glasses and so I was sure to remember where they were."

Parrot sighed the long-suffering sigh of one who had had this sort of problem before.

"Why, what *nice* children you are," said H.H., beaming at them, like a small, fat, Father Christmas. "The boys so handsome and the girl so pretty. My my, and one of each colour, which is so useful because then one can tell you apart – which is such a help when you lose your glasses. Let me see, I must memorise: Penelope, copper-coloured hair; Peter is the one with black curls, yes; and Simon must be the one with blond hair. Yes, yes, I'm sure I shall remember that in a week or two."

"Never mind about that now," said Parrot. "Tell us what's been happening here."

"Well," said H.H. chuckling. "The Cockatrices appeared to be running into a little trouble. They got the right spell for the eggs, of course, which is worrying, but now they've got the Spell Book they've started getting ambitious. But you know how inefficient they always were. Well, they got the spells all muddled up and before they knew where they were they turned two sentries into a bunch of Moon carrots and a small cork-tree that had been struck by lightning."

"Har! har! har!" laughed Parrot, slapping his thigh with his wing. "That's the stuff – what happened then?"

"Well, they came up here and tried to force me to go down and work the spells for them," said H.H. indignantly. "So I retreated in here and they were afraid to follow."

"The thing is," said Parrot, "what are we going to do?"

"Well," said H H., "without the Herbal and the Book of Spells, I can't do anything, as you know. But they've got the three Books of Government down in the dungeons of Cockatrice Castle, so they say, and they're well guarded it seems. I don't see how we're going to get them out; and without them we can't do anything."

"Can't you remember *any* of the spells?" said Parrot.

"No," said H.H. miserably. "When you get to my age, one's memory is not so good. The annoying thing is that I remember distinctly that in the great Book of Spells there is one special spell against Cockatrices, but I can't remember what it is."

"Well," said Parrot, "perhaps it'll come back to you."

"No," said H.H. miserably, "I've tried and tried to remember, but I simply can't."

"Well," said Parrot cheerfully, "don't worry, we'll think of something. Now why don't you run up one of your splendid Moon-carrot meals?"

"Oh, shall I, what fun?" said H.H. "But first I'll take Peter here to soothe Tabitha – she'd like a little feminine company."

"You mean Penelope," said Parrot.

"That's the one with the blond hair, isn't it?" asked H.H.

"No, red hair," said Parrot.

"Yes, yes of course," said H.H. "Well, come along, Penelope my dear."

"Go on," said Parrot. "Tabitha's harmless."

In spite of Parrot's encouragement, Penelope felt very uneasy, as she followed H.H. through the crystal maze. "I put her in the East Wing," panted H.H. "First, it's un-inflammable, and secondly it's sound-proof."

Penelope could see the reason for this as they approached the East Wing. The amount of noise that was being made by an inconsolable Dragon was incredible.

"Boo, *hoo*! Boo, *hoo*! Boo *hoo*!" Penelope heard a voice roaring. "Boo hoo *hoo*! Oh, most stupid and idiotic of dragons that I am. Boo, *hoo*! Oh careless and unintelligent creature that I am. Boo *hoo*!"

H.H. ushered Penelope into a room furnished as a bedroom, and lying on a huge four-poster bed, wracked with sobs, lay the Dragon. She was much smaller than Penelope had imagined, being about the size of a pony. She was a bright sealing-wax pink, decorated along her neck and back with a frill of golden and green scales.

She had huge, china-blue eyes which were awash with tears.

"Now, now, Tabitha," said H.H. "I've brought someone to see you – a girl-child called Penelope."

"How do you do," said Penelope.

"I don't do, that's my trouble. Boo hoo *hoo*!" roared the Dragon, tears running down her cheeks and turning to steam, as they were heated by the flame from her nostrils. "I'm the undoiest Dragon you'd meet in a month of Tuesdays. Boo hoo *hoo*!"

"Perhaps," suggested Penelope gently, "if you tell me about your troubles, it would help. You see, that's what I and my cousins have come here for, to help."

"That's very kind of you," gulped Tabitha, "but I'm alone and forlorn, and nobody can help me, and it's all my fault – Boo hoo *hoo!* and nothing can – Boo *hoo* – be – Boo *hoo* – done – Boo *hoo* – about it – Boo er *hoo*!"

"Nevertheless," said Penelope firmly, "you'd better tell me, just in case. At any rate, crying can't help."

Tabitha pulled out a great handkerchief from under the pillow and blew her nose violently into it, and it immediately caught fire. Penelope and H.H. had to stamp out the flames, much to H.H.'s annoyance. "If I've told her once about using non-inflammable handkerchiefs, I've told her a dozen times," he said. "These flame-producing animals are so careless, you've no idea."

"That's right – boo *hoo*! – be rude to me when my heart is broken – boo *hoo*! and that I'm the last of the Dragons," sobbed Tabitha. "Take it out on me when – boo *hoo*! – I'm weak and defenceless, and the last of my kind."

"Dear me," said H.H. "I never seem to say the right things. Well, I'll leave her with you. If you want anything, ring the bell. Five times for an emergency." He scuttled off and Penelope sat down rather gingerly on the bed beside Tabitha.

"Now Tabitha," she said in a kind but firm voice. "All this crying is only upsetting you and not solving your problems. Now, if you just control yourself and tell me what it's all about I'm sure we can help."

"Well," said Tabitha, taking deep and shuddering breaths, so that the flames flickered out of her nose like little rose petals. "Well, every so often you see all the Dragons vanish, except one, and he or she is the Keeper of the Eggs, which each Dragon lays before vanishing. I was chosen to be the Keeper of the Eggs, and I was so proud because it's a great responsibility to feel you have the whole future of the Dragons in your care, in one basket."

"It must be a great responsibility," said Penelope gravely.

"Well, I was on my way up here with the eggs – they're always hatched out in the Crystal Caves – when I met the Cockatrices to whom I never *normally* speak – they're so *common* and unruly. But they told me that there'd been a change of plan and that they were to take the eggs to Cockatrice Castle for hatching, and I, foolish creature that I am, gave them the eggs; and then – boo hoo *hoo!* – they ran off with them, saying that they were not going to hatch them and that – boo hoo *hoo hoo hoo!* – that there'd be *no more Dragons* . . . WHA! boo *hoo*."

"Cruel beasts," said Penelope angrily, as Tabitha started to sob violently again. "Never you mind, my cousins and I intend to go to Cockatrice Castle and recapture the great Books of Government and your eggs."

"You will? You are?" asked Tabitha. "How?"

"Well," Penelope began, and then stopped. Out of the corner of her eye she'd seen something move in the shadows by the big wardrobe that stood in the corner of the room. "Tell me," she said, "is there anyone else here in the Crystal Caves with you?"

"Anyone else?" said the Dragon, puzzled. "No, only me and H.H. Why?"

Penelope said nothing but she went to the bell and pressed it five times. Within a few seconds there was a pounding of feet and the doors burst open, and Peter and Simon and H.H. rushed in, with Parrot in their wake.

"What's the matter?" cried H.H.

"Yes, what's the trouble?" asked the two boys.

"Close the doors," said Penelope.

They closed the doors and stood looking at her.

"Well?" said Simon.

"We have a spy in our midst," said Penelope calmly. "And he's hiding near the cupboard."

four

✕

SPIES AND PLANS

"A spy, Penny?" asked Peter incredulously. "Are you sure?"

"What sort of a spy?" asked Simon.

"I don't know, I just saw him move. Over there by the wardrobe," said Penelope, pointing.

The two boys strode over to the shadows by the cupboard. "You're quite right," said Peter, and bending down he grabbed at something

" 'Ere, leggo!" said a noarse voice. "Leggo, you're 'urting."

Peter strode back to the others, carrying by one leg a fat, warty, green Toad, wearing a cut-away coat and blonde wig, and holding a grey top hat in its hand. Peter put it on the ground where it crouched, gulping, and gazed at them nervously with its bulbous yellow eyes.

"There you are," said Penelope, triumphantly. "I *told* you there was a spy."

"I'm *not* a spy," said the Toad hoarsely.

"Well, if you're not a spy, what are you?" asked Simon, grimly.

"I'm a . . . I'm . . . a . . . I'm a fur trader from Vladivostock," said the Toad obviously having just thought of it, "and I've gotta wife and six kids wot I've got to support."

"You're nothing of the sort," said Peter, indignantly.

"Don't I *look* like a fur trader from Vladivostock, wot's finding it 'ard to make ends meet?" asked the Toad, plaintively.

"Not a bit," said Simon.

The Toad thought about it for a moment. " 'Ow about a diamond merchant, wot's come all the way from Zulu-land, then?" he asked, brightening.

"You don't look like that, either," said Peter.

"A famous brain-surgeon from Katmandu?" asked the Toad, hopefully.

"No," said Simon.

"Then, I'll tell you the troof," said the Toad earnestly. "I'm a rich dairy farmer from Ontario, wot's on 'oliday and is 'ere visiting 'is niece."

"I don't believe you," said Penelope. "You're a spy."

"I'm not a spy, 'onest I'm not," protested the Toad, " 'onest miss. It's just like wot I was telling you. I'm a very well-to-do corn-merchant wot's travelling incognito to do a bit of business, like."

"You're nothing but a spying Toad," said Peter.

"Yes, and a miserable, ill-favoured Toad at that, wearing a wig and cut-away coat and a ridiculous top-hat," said Simon.

"You got no call to insult me 'at," said the Toad, in a hurt tone of voice. "It's a jolly posh 'at, this is – one of me best disguises – I mean 'ats."

"You're a spy," said Peter. "And you know what happens to spies."

"I'm not a spy, I swear it, I'm not," said the Toad, feverishly. "You can't 'urt me, 'cos I'm *not* a spy."

"Spies get shot," said Simon.

"Or tortured," said Peter.

"Or both," said Parrot, grimly.

" 'Ere! Now steady on! There's no need for that sort of talk," said the Toad, desperately. " 'Ere, look, I'll come clean with you. I didn't want to tell you, but you made me."

"Well?" said Simon.

"I'm a h'exceedingly rich merchant banker of Lithuanian h'extraction, wot's gotta wife, two kids and an ageing old Mum to support," the Toad confessed, tipping his hat over his eyes and sticking his thumbs into his waistcoat.

"I don't believe a word of it," said Penelope.

"Neither do I," said Parrot. "A merchant banker, indeed. A toad like you couldn't add two and two together."

"You don't 'ave to, if you're a banker," the Toad assured him. "'Onest, you don't 'ave to know mathematics and things. It's just looking after people's money for 'em and telling them they can't 'ave it when they want it."

"Rubbish," said Parrot, scornfully. "Unmitigated, unimaginative rubbish. Now, if you don't tell us the truth, we'll get Tabitha here to warm you up with a little flame or two, eh Tabitha?"

"It will be a pleasure," said Tabitha, letting twenty-four smoke rings and two long streams of flame escape from her nostrils.

"Ow! Now, 'ere, that's not fair," said the Toad, his eyes filling with tears. "You can't torture a dumb animal, and me clo's might get burnt and I 'aven't finished paying for 'em yet."

"That's not our concern," said Parrot. "Tell us the truth and we won't harm you."

"'Onest," said the Toad, hopefully. "Crorss your 'eart and spit on your 'and and 'ope to die?"

"Yes," Parrot answered him.

"Well," said the Toad, taking a deep breath. "I'm a ..."

"The truth now," Parrot warned. "It's your last chance."

"Oh, all *right*," said the Toad. "Me name's Ethelred and I'm a Toad of no fixed address."

"And you're a spy?" asked Peter.

"Yes. Well, more of 'alf a spy, like," said Ethelred. "You see it was all the fault of them Cockatrices. I was too small to sit on their eggs for 'em. I kept falling off and 'urting meself. Well, I said to the 'ead Cockatrice, like, I said: 'Why not let me do wot I'm cut out for?' "

"Spying?" said Simon, incredulously. "Why, you're a terrible spy."

"You got no call to insult me like that," said Ethelred, sulkily. "I would have been a jolly good spy but I didn't finish the course."

"What course?" asked Peter.

"Correspondence course in spying wot I was taking," explained Ethelred. "I only got up as far as disguises and foreign accents when the Cockatrices said: ' 'Ere,' they said, 'you nip up to the Crystal Caves and see what H.H. is up to!' they said, and they bundled me out so blooming fast I forgot me invisible ink."

Penelope began to feel quite sorry for him.

"Well," said Parrot, "it's a good thing we caught you, because you can give us some useful information."

"No," said Ethelred, shaking his head. "No, I can't tell you nuffink. Me lips is sealed, like."

Tabitha breathed out two ribbons of flame.

"Well," said Ethelred, hastily, "I could tell you a bit, maybe, the *unimportant* stuff."

"Where have they got the Great Books of Government?" asked H.H. "And are they safe?"

"Cor lummy, yes," said Ethelred. "They've got them down in the dungeons under 'eavy guard. Ooh, they ain't 'alf getting into a pickle with them there spells. Laugh? I nearly died. The tantrum the 'ead Cockatrice 'ad when they turned the two sentries into a tree and a bunch of Moon carrots. Us Toads were 'ysterical, I can tell you."

"And what about the Dragons' eggs?" asked Parrot.

"Oh, they're all right," said Ethelred.

"They're *safe*? In the *Castle*? My precious eggs?" screeched Tabitha, and fainted.

" 'Ere, wot's she on about?' asked Ethelred. "Course, they're safe. Got 'em stacked up in the torture chamber, they 'ave, neat as neat."

They all patted Tabitha's paws until she came round, for, as H.H. wisely observed: "there was no point in burning a feather under her nose, as one did in normal cases for the same thing."

"Now," said Parrot to Ethelred. "What's the best way into the Castle?"

"There *is* only one way in," said H.H., "over the drawbridge and through the big gates."

"That's just where you're all wrong, see?" said Ethelred, triumphantly. "You lot think you know everything, don't you? Well, you're wrong, see?"

"Well, how else can you get in?" asked H.H.

"Ah," said Ethelred, cunningly. "You can't get me to tell you. Ho, no, I'm not one of them turn-abouts."

"Turncoats," said Peter.

"And I'm not one of *those*, neither," said Ethelred.

"I don't believe you," said Penelope. "You've done nothing but tell lies since we caught you, and this is just another lie like telling us you were a brain surgeon. You deliberately lied about who you were and what you were, and now you're lying about there being another way into Cockatrice Castle."

"I'm not lying, miss, swelp me," said Ethelred. "I may have told you a fib or two about who I was, but this is 'onest, 'onest, you get into the Castle by the drains."

"Bravo, Penny," said Peter.

"Most sagacious," said Parrot.

"Brilliant," said H.H.

" 'Ere," protested Ethelred suddenly realising what he had done. "That wasn't very fair, miss, was it, now?"

"Just as fair as you coming to spy on us," said Penelope.

"But that's me *perfession*, master-spy," said Ethelred. "But you 'ad no cause to make me give away a secret."

"Well, I'm sorry. I thought it was necessary," said Penelope, "and nobody will be surprised, because you're a bad spy."

" 'Ere, I don't think that's *fair*, when I'd only done 'alf the course," said Ethelred, pained. "I'm very good really. I can do an 'Ungarian fishmonger with three motherless daughters to the life. Least, that's wot me mum said. Would you like to 'ear me? Or I can do a Polish count wot's fallen on evil times and 'ad to sell 'is castle and whatnot."

"Some other time," said Parrot. "What we want to know now is how do we get into the drains."

" 'Ere," said Ethelred, "you can't expect me to give away *all* the secrets."

"I think," said Penelope, winking at Parrot, "that Ethelred does not realise that we're offering him a very important job."

"Wot, me?" said Ethelred puzzled. "Wot job?"

"Master counter-spy," said Penelope, solemnly.

"Cor, wot *me*?" said Ethelred, his eyes protruding even more with excitement. "Wot's one of them, then?"

"It's the most important kind of spying you can do," said Peter.

"Yes," said Simon. "Frightfully important work."

"Coo," said Ethelred, much impressed. " 'Ow do you do this, then?"

"Well, you go on pretending that you're spying on *us* for the *Cockatrices*," said Penelope, "whereas in *reality* you're spying on the *Cockatrices* for *us*. That's why you'll be called: Master-Counter Spy X."

"*Me?*" asked Ethelred. "Why Master-Counter Spy X? Why can't I use me own name?"

"Because master-counter spies never do," said Peter. "They're much too important to use ordinary names."

Ethelred thought about this for a little bit. "Would I 'ave to use disguises, like?" he asked. "It's just that disguises is one of me better bits, reelly, and I wouldn't like to 'ave to give it up."

"Of course you'll wear disguises," said Penelope, "and most of the time you'll be wearing the most fiendishly cunning disguise of all."

"Wot's that, then?" asked Ethelred, his eyes protruding with eagerness.

"You'll be disguised as yourself," said Penelope, "as a Toad."

"But 'ere, steady on then. Them Cockatrices know I'm a Toad," protested Ethelred.

"That's the fiendishly clever part," said Simon. "Because under the disguise of a Toad you're really Master-Counter Spy X."

"Cor," said Ethelred, understanding dawning on his face. "Cor, that ain't 'alf clever, that is. Coo, that's the most spying bit of spying wot I've ever 'eard of."

The children sighed with relief and Parrot exchanged a glance with H.H.

"So you'll take on this highly important assignment?" asked Penelope.

"Oh yes, miss, please," said Ethelred, his eyes shining. "And may I say, miss, it'll be a pleasure for me to serve with anyone wot's as pretty as wot you are, and 'oo 'as got a master mind like wot I've got."

"Thank you very much," said Penelope, trying not to laugh. "And now if H.H. will be kind enough to give us some food, we can plan our campaign."

So they all went back into the big living-room and Penelope helped H.H. to serve up a delicious meal which consisted of vegetable soup, roast lamb and green peas, baked potatoes stuffed with cream and butter, followed by fresh strawberries encased in whipped cream and meringue and surrounded by ice cream.

"Gosh, that was a splendid meal," said Peter, having had two helpings of the strawberries.

"It's just one of these little banquets that H.H. likes to run up," said Parrot. "He's a very good cook, really. Of course, I must admit that the Moon-carrots help – they're so versatile."

"Yes, you keep mentioning Moon-carrots," said Penelope, "and you were singing about them when we first met. What are they?"

"One of H.H.'s better inventions," said Parrot. "It looks like a red and white striped carrot and we have one crop a year when we have the Moon-carrot gathering ceremony. Then they're hung up to dry."

"When they're dry, they look like this," said H.H. and placed on the table a long carrot-shaped vegetable which was hard, like a gourd. As they dry, the instructions start to appear. Look!" On the side of the Moon-carrot the children could see, written in neat Gothic script with a lot of twirls and squiggles, the legend: *Roast leg of Pork – empty contents into casserole and put in a two-log oven for two hours. Baste frequently.* Breaking open the Moon-carrot, H.H. showed them the contents were a brownish powder.

"Do you mean to say that everything we've just eaten came from that?" asked Simon, incredulously.

"Yes," said H.H., modestly.

"And it's not like ordinary tinned or dried packet stuff," said Parrot, "because this is actually grown in the ground, so it's lost none of its goodness."

"Incredible," said Peter.

"H.H. invented that in 1596," said Parrot. "He was always ahead of his time with his inventions."

"I really think you're the most marvellous magician," said Penelope. "All your inventions are so *practical*."

"Well, well, that's kind of you," said H.H., blushing a little, "but we must give most of the credit to the Great Books. Without them, I can do very little."

"Yes, so it's essential that we get them back," said

Parrot. "Now let's map out our campaign. First, where's that plan of Cockatrice Castle?"

"I have it here," said H.H., pulling a roll of parchment from his robes. They spread it out on the table and pored over it.

"Now, Ethelred, my lad," said Parrot. "Where's this drain you're talking about?"

Ethelred frowned over the plan, gulping with concentration, his wig perched slightly over one eye, his hat on the back of his head. "Well, 'ere's the drawbridge," he said at last, "and 'ere's the Chief Cockatrice's living quarters, and *'ere* are the barracks where the rest of 'em 'ang out. Then down 'ere is the main dungeon where they've got the Great Books; 'ere's the torture chamber where they've got the eggs."

"My lovely eggs," squeaked Tabitha.

"Now, don't go fainting again," said Parrot, testily. "We haven't time to waste giving you first-aid."

"Now 'ere," Ethelred went on, jabbing at the plan with his thumb, " 'ere are the two smaller dungeons, wot are never used, except for storage. I was sent down there one day, to get a chair, and I found this sort of drain thing, see? So I went along it, just for a lark, like, and I found it went under the moat and came out in the fields over 'ere. So I says to meself, I says, Ethelred, I says, mark my words, that'll come in useful some time – and it 'as." Ethelred beamed at them happily.

"I think that was very clever of you," said Penelope, admiringly.

Ethelred blushed to the roots of his wig.

"Now," said Simon, frowning at the map. "If we get in *here*, we've still got to get to the sentries and deal with them before we can rescue the Books."

"You can't rescue the Books," said Parrot, gloomily. "At least not this way. Each book weighs about three hundred pounds and measures six feet by three."

"Good heavens," said Peter. "Why didn't you tell us?"

"But my dear Parrot," said H.H., "they don't have to *rescue* the Books, they can just get the recipe for dealing with Cockatrices, which I've so stupidly forgotten, and then we can drive the Cockatrices out of the Castle and rescue the Books."

"Of course," said Simon, excitedly, "you're quite right, H.H. If we can get in and get the right spell, that's all we need."

"Now all we have to think of is a way of frightening the guards," said Peter. "What frightens Cockatrices?"

"Are you joking, mister?" asked Ethelred, incredulously. "Nothing frightens that lot; they don't 'ave to be frightened if they can spit out flames eight feet long."

"He's quite right," said Parrot. "Cockatrices have always been arrogant and ambitious animals."

There was a long silence, broken only by Dulcibelle humming to herself, as she re-made Parrot's bed.

"Well," said Penelope at last. "If we can't frighten them, what about luring them away, somehow?"

"Not the Cockatrices," said H.H. "They've a really military discipline, you know, which means that none of the sentries thinks for himself, he merely obeys orders. And once they're told to guard a place, they guard it no matter what."

There was another silence.

"Tell you wot," said Ethelred suddenly. "There's one thing wot might make 'em shift."

"What?" said everyone eagerly.

"Well," said Ethelred. "The 'ead Cockatrice, 'e said to everyone that it was their duty, like, to catch H.H., and 'e said that the one wot 'elped to capture H.H. would get promotion. If they saw H.H. and thought they could catch 'im, that might shift 'em."

"An excellent idea if H.H. had been two hundred years

younger," said Parrot, dryly, "but at his age you can't expect him to go crawling about in drains and running away from Cockatrices."

"I am sorry to say so, but I must admit that Parrot is right," said H.H. in a depressed tone of voice.

"Well then, how about a fake H.H.?" asked Simon.

There was another silence while everybody looked at each other.

"You mean a sort of model?" asked Penelope.

"Yes," said Simon. "You know, something dressed up to look like H.H. One of us, maybe."

"No, no," said H.H. "I think I've got it. When I last had some robes made, they made a sort of dummy of me to fit the robes on."

"A tailor's dummy," breathed Penelope delightedly.

"That's it," said H.H. excitedly. "Now we've got that, which is the right size and shape, and I've got a spare hat and robes to dress it in."

"Make a face out of Moon-calf jelly," shouted Simon.

"Paint it to look like H.H.," yelled Peter.

"And if that doesn't fetch them guards running, nuffink will," yelled Ethelred, his hat falling off as he did a wild hopping dance round the table.

"Wait a minute, wait a minute," said Parrot, "that's all very well but how do we do it?"

" 'Ere's 'ow," said Ethelred, so bursting with excitement that his cut-away coat was straining at the seams. "Wheels, that's wot."

"Wheels?" said everybody, looking mystified.

"Yes," said Ethelred. "Where's that plan?"

He pored over the plan for a moment and then sat back with a satisfied smile on his face. "Yes, that's it," he said.

"What?" asked everybody.

"Well," said Ethelred, leaning over the plan and showing them with his thumb. " 'Ere's the two dungeons wot 're used as store-rooms, see, and that 's the one we come out into."

"Yes," said Parrot. "Go on."

"Well, 'ere we 'ave the dungeon wot 'as got the Books in," said Ethelred, "and right opposite it is a long corridor wot slopes down to the moat."

"Of course," said H.H., slapping his forehead. "That's where you go to check on the water level in the moat. How silly of me to forget it."

"At the bottom of this 'ere corridor," Ethelred went on, "there's the moat, see."

"I don't understand," said Peter.

"Well, we comes into this dungeon 'ere, see," said Ethelred, "and then I goes out and attracts the guards' attention like."

"You create a diversion," said Parrot.

"No," said Ethelred, "fair's fair. I don't want to do anything dangerous. No, I'll simply attract their attention and while their attention is attracted you can go and put the model of H.H. 'ere at the top of the corridor and give it a shove. Then if it goes running off down on its wheels, I shall say: 'Coo, look, lummy,' I shall say, 'isn't that H.H.,' and then they'll all go chasing after 'im, see."

"What a splendid idea," said Simon, enthusiastically.

"Yes," said Peter, looking at Ethelred with respect. "He really is turning out to be a Master-Counter Spy."

"Still, we've got a long way to go before we're successful," said Parrot worriedly.

"Look, let's divide up the work," said Simon. "Ethelred, H.H. and I will look at this plan and work out the measurements and things, so that we get it just right. You, Parrot and Peter and Penelope do the model with the help of Tabitha and Dulcibelle. What's the best time for our attack, do you think?"

"The middle of the night," said H.H. He pulled out a large watch from under his robes. "That gives us six hours. To make sure it's dark, I'll switch off the moon."

"Can you?" asked Penelope in astonishment.

"Oh yes," said H.H. proudly. "Easily. I can switch off the sun, too, in an emergency."

"Right, then we'd better get started," said Peter. "Come on, Parrot, show me where the Moon-calf jelly is kept."

The next three hours were full of activity. Ethelred, H.H. and Simon drew the dungeon entrance and the sloping corridor in chalk on the floor and they worked out how it was best to manoeuvre the model into place. Tabitha and Dulcibelle, not without a certain amount of argument and rivalry, arranged the robes on the dummy which had already been attached to wheels made out of Moon-calf jelly. But it was the model of H.H.'s head that took the time. Six models were made and rejected before they got one that they considered perfect. Then, with great care, Penelope painted it with oil paint; they stuck a false beard and hair on it, attached it to the model and put a pointed hat on it; and stood back. There was a long silence broken at last by Ethelred.

"Coo, lummy," he said in a hushed whisper. "If that ain't H.H. to the life. It's just like his blinking twin brother. If that don't fool 'em, nuffink will."

"I must say," said Parrot, judiciously, "I think he's right. Even I might mistake it for H.H. It's a deliciously deceiving doppelgänger."

"Coo, you don't 'alf go on when you start," said Ethelred, admiringly. "I don't know 'ow you remember all them words."

"You had your chance to have a command over the language," said Parrot austerely, "when H.H. started his Free School for Toads. But would any of you attend? No! you preferred sitting about in swamps, singing and doing part-time egg hatching for the Cockatrices, and doing *both* things badly."

"It wasn't my fault, 'onest," pleaded Ethelred. "I *wanted*

to come to school, but my mum said there was no sense in all that learning rubbish. She said I ought to take up a trade, like."

"So what did you do?" asked Penelope, feeling sorry for him.

"Well, I took up spying, didn't I? Me mum said: 'There's always room for a good spy,' " said Ethelred.

Parrot gave a heartfelt sigh. "They're all the same, these Toads," he muttered, "no logic."

"Now," said Simon, "let's go over the plan of campaign. The ones to go on this expedition are Peter, myself, Parrot and, of course, Ethelred to act as guide and Master-Counter Spy."

"Here," said Penelope, "what about me?"

"You'd far better stay here with me, my dear," said H.H. "After all, it's a dangerous mission."

"I don't care," said Penelope, stubbornly. "I'm going with them. After all, I tricked Ethelred into telling you about the drain, otherwise you wouldn't be going at all."

"That's perfectly true," said Peter, uneasily.

"Well, all right, you can come," said Simon, "but only if you promise to run like a rabbit at the first sign of danger."

"I shall not," said Penelope with dignity. "I shall only run like a rabbit when everyone *else* runs like a rabbit."

"I think we can make sure that Penelope's safe," said Parrot. "Now, what do we all do?"

"Well," said Simon, "when we get into the dungeon *here*, Ethelred goes out and creates a diversion."

" 'Ere, I told you I'm not doing one of them," interrupted Ethelred. "I just attract the guards' attention."

"All right," said Simon, smiling. "Once Ethelred's enticed the guards into the dungeon, where the Books are, then we go out and put the model into this corridor *here*, and Parrot says he will sit on its shoulders and imitate H.H.'s voice. *Then*, when Ethelred tells the guard that it's

H.H., Parrot will fly off the model and give it a push with his feet, and it will then go rolling down the corridor and into the moat. With luck, the guards will follow it, and maybe even dive for it, because we weighted it so that when it hits the water it'll sink. While all this is happening, we go in to the Books and ask about the cure for Cockatrices and Penelope writes it down. Then we escape."

"Splendid, simply splendid," said H.H. "What a masterly plan. How grateful I am to you brave children."

" 'Ere, what about me?" said Ethelred, hurt.

"You've proved yourself to be a truly sagacious and intelligent Toad," said H.H., patting him on his top hat. "And when this is all over, I'll make you Head Toad at the Free School for Toads."

"Cor," said Ethelred, overcome with the honour.

"Now, I think we all ought to have a hot drink of Moon-carrot cocoa and then I'll go and switch off the moon and you can go," said H.H.

"One thing wot's worrying me," said Ethelred, sipping his cocoa, "that is, should I stay on as Master-Counter spy X, or should I escape with you lot?"

"Escape with us," said Penelope, firmly. "The Cockatrices will know that you've changed sides. Besides, we'll have plenty of other important work for you to do."

"Just say the word, miss," said Ethelred, tipping his hat over one eye in a devil-may-care manner. "Just you say the word and Master-Counter Spy X is at your service."

"Thank you," said Penelope, gravely.

When they'd finished the cocoa, which was very warm and stomach-comforting, H.H. consulted his watch. "Time for me to put out the moon," he said. "Are you all ready?"

"*Yes*," said everyone.

"Good luck," said Tabitha and Dulcibelle, both sniffing violently into their handkerchiefs.

So the party set off down one of the many side tunnels of the Crystal Caves – one that would bring them out within a short distance of the Moon-carrot field where lay the entrance to the drain. Penelope and Ethelred, carrying torches, went first with Parrot, and Peter and Simon brought up the rear, carrying the model of H.H. At last they left the tunnel and made their way out into the field, which, without a moon, was as black as the bottom of a well. It was very silent and they could hear the whisper of the Moon-carrot leaves, soft as velvet, brushing against their ankles. They only used the torches when absolutely necessary, especially when they neared the great, dark bulk of Cockatrice Castle, just in case a sentry should spot them and give the alarm.

"Stop 'ere a minute," whispered Ethelred. "It's somewhere 'ere. I'll 'ave to look for it."

So Parrot and the children waited while Ethelred hopped about among the Moon-carrot leaves, muttering to himself. " 'Ere it is," he said at last. "I knew it was 'ere somewhere."

With their torches, the children could see a square manhole with a wire cover lying beside it. Shining their torches into it, they could see it led into a large, circular, brick built drain. Just under the manhole was a chair.

"That's 'ow I got out," said Ethelred proudly.

Carefully they lowered themselves and the dummy down into the drain, and here things became easier, since they could shine their torches without fear of being seen. After walking for about five minutes, the tunnel sloped downwards and they could feel a cool breeze on their faces.

"Nearly there," whispered Ethelred. "Dead quiet now. Them guards are only just round the corner."

He led them out of the drain into a great, grim dungeon piled high with old furniture, candelabras, and all the other strange things that are generally found in an attic, all dusty and hung with cobwebs as thick as black lace. The who e place had a cold, damp smell that made Penelope shiver. Ethelred led them through the great piles of cobweb-covered furniture until they came to the door and this he opened a crack and peered through. " 'Ere, 'ave a look and get the lie of the land," he said at last.

Each of them in turn peered through the crack. A little way down the passage was the big, arched door bound in brass, which obviously led to the dungeon where the Great Books of Government were held, for, lounging outside the door, were two bored-looking Cockatrices who were obviously sentries. One was busy sharpening his great claws with his beak, while the other one was amusing himself by cutting his initials in the wall with the flames from his nostrils. Opposite to them was the corridor which sloped down towards the moat.

"Now," said Ethelred, his voice shaking with a mixture of alarm and excitement, "when I get them two into the dungeon, you get the model in place and then Parrot can say something loud, so that I'll know you're ready, see?"

"Yes," everyone whispered.

Penelope could feel her heart hammering inside her ribs and she wondered if the others felt as scared as she did.

"Well," said Ethelred, gulping, " 'ere we go then."

So saying, he opened the door, slipped into the corridor and half closed the door behind him. The others, their eyes glued to the crack, saw him straighten his hat and with a jaunty air hop down the corridor towards the sentries, carrying Penelope's pencil and pad under his arm.

" 'Ere," he shouted. "Show a leg there. Call yourselves sentries? I could 'ave crept up and strangled you both."

The Cockatrices, at the sound of his voice, had leapt

97

T.P.—D

to attention, but they relaxed when they saw who it was.

"Oh, it's you, is it," said one of them, in a nasty, harsh, crowy voice, that sounded something like a dog worrying a bone. "What do you want, you stupid Toad?"

"I want no lip out of *you*, for a start," said Ethelred, sternly. "I'll thank you to keep a civil tongue in your ugly face, because I just came down 'ere on a special mission from your Chief, see; and if you don't believe me why don't you nip upstairs and ask 'im. I wouldn't advise it because he's in a bad temper like a volcano wot's going to erupt, see."

"What's wrong with him?" asked the sentries, in alarm.

It was obvious from their uneasy attitude that when the Chief Cockatrice was in a temper everyone suffered.

"H.H. is the matter," said Ethelred. "Yes, that's what it is: H.H. planning vengeance on us all."

"How can he?" sneered the Cockatrices. "We've got all his Books here. He hasn't any spells left."

"All right then," said Ethelred triumphantly. "If 'e 'asn't any spells left, 'ow 'as 'e managed to *put out the moon*?"

"Put out the *moon*?" echoed the sentries, incredulously.

"Yes," said Ethelred. "If you don't believe me, go up on the battlements and look. That's why your Chief's dead scared, 'e is. That's why 'e 'as sent me down 'ere to look up moon spells in the Great Book of Spells, and that's why I 'aven't time to stand 'ere gossiping with you lot. Open that door and let me in, or you'll both catch it in the neck from the Chief."

"Of course, of course," said one of the sentries, hastily, taking a giant key off the wall and unlocking the door.

"And you'd better both come in with me and lend an 'and," said Ethelred.

"Of course, of course," said the sentries, following him obediently as he hopped into the dungeon.

"Now," said Peter, "stay here, Penny, until the sentries chase the model."

He and Simon opened the door and hurriedly wheeled the model of H.H. down the corridor as quietly as they could. In the dungeon they heard Ethelred keeping the sentries occupied.

"Now, you 'old me pad, and you 'old me pencil," he said. "This 'ere's a serious business, putting out the moon. The next thing you know 'e'll put out the sun – then where will we be, eh?"

Carefully and rapidly, the twins arranged the model at the top of the slope where the slightest touch would send it careering down the corridor. Then Parrot took up his position on its shoulder.

"All right," he whispered, "get back inside and under cover."

As soon as Parrot saw they were safely out of sight, he shuffled all his feathers into position and cleared his throat. "My dear Parrot," he said, in a remarkable imitation of H.H.'s piping voice, "this putting out of the moon is only the first step in my campaign against the Cockatrices."

"Really," said Parrot in his own voice. "What's the next step?"

"Cor! lummy! Bless my socks and topper!" screamed Ethelred from inside the dungeon. "Look! H.H. 'imself. Quick, catch 'im. It means promotion, 'uge medals. The Chief will love you. Quick, quick, quick."

The sentries turned, bewildered, and then they saw what they took to be H.H. standing in the corridor with Parrot on his shoulder. It took them a second or so to recover from their shock. But then, with crows of triumph, they leapt forward.

"Look out, H.H., Cockatrices," screamed Parrot in pretended alarm, and he flew off the model's shoulder, giving it a kick with his feet as he did so.

The model twirled round and then started to roll down the corridor, gathering speed. The long robes swept the ground so the wheels were completely hidden and the impression of H.H. running for his life down the corridor was so good it would have deceived anyone, let alone a pair of Cockatrices. Gobbling with eagerness to catch H.H., the Cockatrices, jostling each other, rushed down the corridor in pursuit of the model.

"All clear," called Parrot. "Quick as you can."

The children ran out of the dungeon and into the one where Ethelred was waiting for them.

" 'Ere," he said, "you get the blinking spells and I'll keep watch for the Cockatrices."

He hopped out of the dungeon and down the corridor where the sentries had disappeared.

Then the children saw the Great Books of Government, each six feet long by three feet wide, and made from the most exquisitely tooled leather, picked out in patterns of scarlet and gold. Each Book lay on a beautifully constructed golden table inlaid with silver.

"Hallo, Books," said Parrot, affectionately.

To the children's surprise, the Books answered in musical voices that sounded like three little old ladies.

"Hallo, there you are, Parrot," they said. "It *is* nice to see you again. Are you going to rescue us?"

"Not this time," said Parrot. "We're getting around to it, my lovely loquacious library. No, what we've come for is a spell against Cockatrices, if you'd be so kind, Spell Book."

To the children's astonishment, the Book marked 'Ye Greate Booke of Spells' opened itself and started to riffle its pages, murmuring to itself.

"Cockatrice . . . Cockatrice," said the Book, "I don't recall off hand . . . Cockatrice . . . I may be wrong, of course . . ."

"I say, get a move on," said Parrot, "those guards may be back in a moment."

"I'm doing it as fast as I can," said the Book, aggrievedly. "I've only got one set of pages. Let's see now – Cockatrice . . . Cockatrice."

The children and Parrot were in an agony of suspense. They had no means of knowing how long the model H.H. would keep the sentries busy and they had no desire to be caught by the angry and frustrated Cockatrices on their return.

"Ha, yes, here we are," said the Great Book of Spells in a pleased tone of voice. "The Spell to Rid Yourself of Cockatrice."

"Are you ready to write it down, Penelope?" asked Parrot.

"Yes," said Penelope.

"Right, here we go," said the Book.

"Recipe for the overcoming of Cockatrice.
Cockatrice are overcome by Weasels. Men
bring Weasels to the den where the Cockatrice
lurketh and is hid, for no things have been
left without remedy. And so the Cockatrice
fleeth when he seeth the Weasel, and the
Weasel pursueth and slayeth him, for the
biting of the Weasel is death to the
Cockatrice, but this only if the Weasel eat
rue before. And against such venom, first
the Weasel eateth the herb of rue. They be
bitten by virtue of the juice of that herb.
He goeth boldly forth and overcometh his
enemy."

"What on earth is rue?" asked Peter.

"It seems to be a sort of plant, I should think," said the Spell Book. "Ask the Dictionary."

The Great Dictionary opened itself and riffled its pages. "Let's see," it said to itself. "Let's see: Rud, rudder, ruddock, ruddy, rude, ruderal, Rüdesheimer, rudiment, rue – here we are – 'A strong smelling, shrubby plant, with pinnately divided leaves and greenish-yellow flowers, symbolic of repentance, compunction or compassion.' You'd better ask the Herbal where it grows."

Thus appealed to, Hepsibar's Herbal opened *its* covers and riffled *its* pages. "Er, rue, rue," it said. "Here we are: 'Rue in the Country of Mythologia grows only in a clearing near the Mandrake Forest, Werewolf Island, in the Singing Sea.' "

"Good." said Parrot, "Got all that, Penelope? Well, H.H. will be able to make some sense of it. Good-bye, Books, and it won't be long before we rescue you."

At that moment the door burst open and Ethelred hopped in very out of breath. " 'Ere, get a *move* on," he panted. "Them sentries 'ave been diving for H.H. and they're coming back all dripping wet. They're as mad as mad, 'cos they know they've been fooled. We must get out of here quick."

They all rushed out of the dungeon, and there, coming up the corridor from the moat, came the two dripping sentries. As soon as the two Cockatrices saw the children, they uttered a terrible crowing, yarring cry that echoed a thousand times from the walls of the corridor, almost deafening Penelope and the boys.

"Quick, quick," cried Parrot. "Back to the drain, run for your lives."

As Ethelred would never be able to keep up, Penelope picked him up in her arms and carried him clasped tightly to her, as she ran faster than she had ever run in her life before. They could hear the gobbling of the Cockatrices, the clattering of their scales and the screech of their claws on the stone floor. Any minute Penelope expected to feel a blast of agonising flame envelop her, but they managed to reach a small dungeon and rush inside and slam the door and bolt it, just as the first blast of flame from the Cockatrices licked round the door frame. They rushed over to the corner where the entrance to the drain was, and they could hear the Cockatrices screaming, like cats, with rage, scraping and tearing at the dungeon door with their claws. They lowered themselves into the drain and scurried along it, climbed out, ran through the field of Moon-carrots and did not really stop to draw breath until they were safely inside the Crystal Caves again.

"Whew!" said Penelope, leaning against a crystal wall and gasping for breath. "I never want to have to run that fast again."

"Nor I," gasped Peter, his chest heaving.

"That was a close thing," said Simon, gulping for air. "We only just got that door closed in time, otherwise we'd have all been burnt to toast."

"Oh, don't," said Penelope, shuddering. "It was horrible."

" 'Ere, miss," said Ethelred, who still lay in Penelope's arms, wearing his top hat. " 'Ere, miss, I'd like to thank you for saving me life."

"Nonsense," said Penelope, putting him on the ground. "I only picked you up, because I didn't think you could hop as fast as we could run."

"And I *couldn't* 'ave, miss," said Ethelred earnestly. " 'Onest, I'd 'ave been a roast Toad, if it 'adn't been for you. Grateful I am, miss, very grateful indeed."

"Well, let's get back to H.H.," said Parrot, "and see if he can make head or tail of this spell. I'm sure I can't. It's too confusing."

So having regained their breath, they made their way back through the crystal tunnels to where H.H., Tabitha and Dulcibelle anxiously awaited their return.

"You're back! You're back! Thank goodness," cried H.H. when he saw them. "Were you successful, you brave creatures?"

"Highly successful," chortled Parrot. "*Very* highly successful."

"And was the model of any use?" asked H.H. eagerly.

"The model was what you might call an electrifying effigy," said Parrot.

"We've got the spell," said Penelope, handing H.H. her little note book. "Though whether it will make any sense to you, I don't know."

"Well now, well now," said H.H., adjusting his glasses and sitting down. "Let me just study it a minute."

They watched him as he read the instructions, his lips moving silently.

"Did you see my eggs?" whispered Tabitha.

"No," said Penelope, "but we saw that they were *very* safely locked up."

"Well," said Tabitha, sighing. "I suppose that's something."

"This is most interesting," said H.H. at last. "Most curious spell indeed. Now, who would have thought of Weasels as a method of getting rid of Cockatrices?"

"Certainly not me," said Parrot. "Never thought much of the Weasels – dull, decadent lot, eccentric and effeminate. The only reason for getting them on our side is that there're a lot of them. How many were there at the last count, H.H.?"

"Seven hundred and seventy-seven," said H.H.

"Why, if we got them on our side, that would be splendid," said Peter, his eyes shining.

"Yes, with the Unicorns, surely we'd be strong enough to attack?" said Simon.

"Har! har! har!" laughed Parrot. "Har! har har! ho ho ho! pardon me, but the very idea of Weasels *fighting*, Har! har! har!"

"But what's so funny about it?" asked Penelope. "I mean there're seven hundred and seventy-seven of them, surely they'd be of some help? What's wrong with them?"

"Wrong with them? Why they're a pack of lay-about cissies, that's what," said Ethelred. "They'd be as much use in a fight as a bunch of over-ripe bananas."

"A vulgar way of putting it," said Parrot. "But I'm afraid he's right. The Weasels have as much fight in them as a handful of apple blossom."

"However," said H.H., "we must not overlook the business of the rue. It's a plant that I've had little to do with, but according to this it seems to make the Weasels become . . . um . . . um . . ."

"Belligerent?" suggested Parrot.

"Just so, belligerent," said H.H., "enough to attack Cockatrices. Now if this is true, and one cannot doubt the Great Books, there must be some reference to it in the History of Weaseldom."

"But if this rue stuff really does make the Weasels bellig . . . bellig . . . what you said," said Penelope, "then why don't we just go and *get* some and make them eat it, and then join us." H.H. pulled his spectacles down to the end of his nose and frowned at her.

"That's all very well, my dear," he said. "The rue grows only on Werewolf Island, and that is a very long voyage from here and, moreover, one of the most unsafe and unpleasant bits of Mythologia, and there's no point in going on such a long and dangerous journey to collect the rue unless we are sure that the Weasels will eat it. It says here that it is bitter. I'm sure they wouldn't like *that*. Although I suppose I could add sugar."

"Surely the first thing to do is to contact the Weasels," suggested Simon. "If we explained to them how dangerous the Cockatrices are getting, surely they'd help."

"I very much doubt it," said Parrot, gloomily.

"So do I," said H.H. "But I suppose it's worth trying."

"How far away do the Weasels live?" asked Penelope.

"Oh, not very far," said Parrot, "about five miles away, on a very nice promontory in the Bottle Forest. They call it Weaseldom, the silly creatures."

"Well," said Penelope, "what I suggest is that we all try to get some sleep, and then tomorrow morning we go and see the Chief Weasel or whatever he's called."

"Duke Wensleydale," said Parrot, with a snort. "Stupid animal."

"Well, Duke Wensleydale, then," said Penelope. "I'm sure if we talked to him, we could persuade him."

As no one could think of a better plan, they all went rather gloomily to bed.

Penelope lay awake for a long time, worrying over the whole problem. The chief difficulty seemed to be that all the creatures in Mythologia were so disorganised, so that naturally the Cockatrices – who were well organised – were gaining the day, but she felt sure that if they could only get the Weasels on their side they could capture Cockatrice Castle. With this comforting thought she fell asleep.

Early the next morning the three children set out on their private Unicorns, accompanied by Parrot, who rode on Penelope's shoulder, and Ethelred who rode behind Penelope, holding on to her very tightly and trying to pretend he wasn't afraid. At first they rode through the Cork Forests, then they came to a most curious type of country. Here the red rocks were heaped up higgledy piggledy on top of one another in tall, tottering piles, and in between them grew the most extraordinary-looking trees, the trunks of which were shaped like long-necked wine bottles.

"Bottle Trees," explained Parrot, when Peter remarked on them. "Another of H.H.'s inventions. The trunks are hollow and water-tight. You just simply choose the right size bottle you want, trim the branches off, and there you are. On the way home you can cut yourself a cork to fit it."

"I really do think H.H. is extraordinary the way he thinks of these things," said Penelope, admiringly.

"Oh, that's nothing," said Parrot airily. "Over on the north-east we've got two sorts of box hedges."

"Two sorts?" asked Simon.

"Yes," said Parrot, "cardboard and wooden. Just pluck the sizes you want straight off the hedge. All with lids of course."

By this time the path had led them on to a promontory high on the hills from which there was a wonderful view over Mythologia, lying misty in the dawn below them, and the great, golden shining sea with its cluster of islands dotted about as far as the eye could see.

"This is Weaseldom," said Parrot, with a wave of his wing. "In many ways one of the nicest parts of Mythologia. I keep telling H.H. he ought to build himself a little weekend cottage up here. The Weasels wouldn't mind."

They wended their way through the groups of Bottle Trees and round a great tottering pile of rock. Then, there in front of them, with his back towards them, stood a Weasel sentry, holding a very large, cumbersome-looking spear over his shoulder. He was dressed in a blue velvet uniform with brass buttons and on his head was a hat with a long, green feather in it.

"Ahoy there!" shouted Parrot. "Ahoy!"

The effect on the Weasel was immediate. He leapt almost his own height in the air, dropped his spear, uttered a piercing shriek and leant back against the rocks, with his eyes closed and a hand to his heart.

"I give in," he screamed. "I surrender. I'll give you anything, I tell you anything. Only please, *please* don't harm me."

"Silly creature, it's me, Parrot," said Parrot.

"If you don't harm me, the Duke will reward you," the Weasel babbled on, his eyes still firmly shut. "My mother and father will reward you . . . my aunt will reward you . . . my three nephews will reward you . . ."

"You infuriating, idiotic beast," shouted Parrot. "It's *me*, Parrot."

"What?" said the Weasel, his eyes still closed. "Parrot?"

"Yes," said Parrot. "Don't keep *on* so."

The Weasel opened one eye cautiously and then he opened both eyes and blinked.

"It really is you, Parrot," he said. "But what are those creatures you've got with you?"

"Children," said Parrot

"Do they bite?" asked the Weasel in a trembling voice, picking up his spear and pointing it at Penelope and the boys. "If they bite, I don't want to have anything to do with them. Tell them I shall fight to the death. Tell them how sharp my spear is. Tell them what a temper I've got when aroused."

"They're perfectly harmless, you ninny," said Parrot, impatiently. "Now let us by, we're here to see Wensleydale."

"Pass friends, all's well," said the sentry in a trembling voice. "Second on the left by the next pile of rocks."

"I must say, I do see what you mean about them not being very *brave*," said Peter as they rode on.

"Yes," said Simon. "It would take an awful lot of rue to make *that* sentry fight."

They rounded another great pile of rocks and suddenly came upon a sight that made them all gasp with surprise. A large flat area had been cleared and laid out like a formal garden with carefully-kept hedges and neatly-raked gravel paths, beautifully-weeded flower beds ablaze with flowers, fountains and ornamental lakes. In the middle of it stood a lovely, half-timbered Elizabethan house with beams as black as jet, snow-white walls and a tiled roof, twisted chimney pots in the deepest of fox red. The numerous windows glittered and gleamed in the sunlight. If you were to come across it in the English countryside, you would have thought it a remarkable old house, but to find it suddenly in the curious landscape of Mythologia was extraordinary. What made it even more surprising was the whole thing was in miniature. The hedges were only six inches high and the fountains the size of a wash basin, and the house itself was like a gigantic doll's house.

"Har," chuckled Parrot at the children's astonishment. "Surprised, eh? Well, it's a nice enough house in its way. Weasel Court, residence of Wensleydale, the Duke of Weaseldom."

"Why is he called Wensleydale?" asked Simon.

"His father was devoted to cheese," explained Parrot. "He actually wanted to call him Gorgonzola, but his mother put her foot down. Great eaters the Weasels. Now, we'd better leave the Unicorns here. We don't want them stamping all over the garden with their great hooves."

So the children got down from the Unicorns and picked their way carefully through the beautifully tended gardens.

"Ain't 'alf posh, miss," said Ethelred, rather overawed by his surroundings. "Wouldn't mind 'aving a 'ouse like this meself."

"It's lovely," agreed Penelope.

Parrot marched up to the front step, lifted the knocker with his beak and knocked loudly.

"Go away," screamed a shrill voice from behind the door. "Go away! There's not a *soul* at home, so there. And all valuables have been transported to the mountains, *and* there are fifty blood-thirsty Weasels armed to the teeth guarding the house. *And* there's nobody here, so go away."

"Wensleydale, stop being a nincompoop," shouted Parrot. "It's me, Parrot, I want to talk to you."

"Parrot," said the voice. "Parrot? Are you sure?"

"Of course I'm sure," said Parrot exasperated.

"How do I know you're Parrot?" asked the voice.

"Would I say I am Parrot if I wasn't?" asked Parrot.

"You're *absolutely* right," said the voice. "That hadn't occurred to me."

"Well, open the door," said Parrot.

There was the sound of a great many keys jangling, bolts being withdrawn, bars removed, and then at last the door opened and out came Wensleydale, the Duke of Weaseldom. He wore a scarlet velvet coat and knee breeches, scarlet hat with a curling yellow feather and he had a great deal of lace at his throat and his cuffs. He was followed by his wife who was most attractively dressed in a pale mauve crinoline and wore a diamond tiara between her neat little ears.

"Why," said Penelope, in astonishment, "they're white. I thought all weasels were brown."

"No, miss," Ethelred explained, "he and she is ermine. Them's haristocrats of Weaseldom. They're all white and all the dukes and such, and all the common Weasels is brown."

"Oh, I see," said Penelope.

Meanwhile, Wensleydale had embraced Parrot with every symptom of delight.

"My *dear* fellow," he said. "My *very* dear fellow. How

wonderful to see you alive and well. We heard the most *dreadful* stories about what had happened to you. How the Cockatrices had burnt you up and stolen the Great Books and turned H.H. into a very small and insignificant cloud. And, of *course* my dear, we were simply *incensed*, weren't we, Winifred?"

"Yes," said Winifred. "I've never known him so incensed."

"Black with fury, I was, I do assure you. Shaking with *uncontrollable rage*, wasn't I, Winnie?"

"Yes, Wensleydale," said Winifred. "Uncontrollable."

" 'I must go with my trusty followers and put these ignorant Cockatrices in their place,' I said, pounding the table and frothing at the mouth, didn't I, Winnie?"

"Yes, Wensleydale," said Winifred, "frothing."

" 'I will give them a thrashing they'll *never* forget,' I said, a *'regular trouncing'*, didn't I, Winnie?"

"Yes, Wensleydale," said Winifred, "trouncing."

" 'Every Cockatrice will be black and blue,' I vowed, 'if I have to do it with my *bare paws*,' didn't I, Winnie?"

"Yes, Wensleydale," said Winifred, "with bare paws."

"Well, I'm glad you feel like that," said Parrot, "because that's what we've come to see you about – fighting the Cockatrices."

Wensleydale immediately bent over double and clasped his hip. "My dear fellow," he gasped, "as I was telling you, I would have been down there now, beating the Cockatrices into a *pulp*, my dear boy – into a pulp – but I was stricken with my lumbago again, wasn't I Winnie?"

"Yes, Wensleydale," said Winifred, "lumbago."

"I didn't know you suffered from lumbago?" said Parrot.

"*Martyr* to it, my dear boy," said Wensleydale. "Positively, a martyr to it. When it attacks I can't move at all. The pain is *agonising*, my dear fellow – simply *agonising*. But

I'm terribly brave about the whole thing, aren't I, Winnie?"

"Yes, Wensleydale," said Winifred, "terribly brave."

"Ironing your back with a hot iron is supposed to be good for lumbago," suggested Penelope.

"Ow! They talk!" said Wensleydale in alarm, backing into the front door. "What are they, Parrot?"

"Children," said Parrot.

"Do they bite?" asked Wensleydale, faintly. "If they do, keep them on their leashes. You never know if you're bitten by one of those things what you might catch."

"Don't be silly," said Parrot. "They're here to help us. But, we must have *your* help or we can't overthrow the Cockatrices."

"My dear fellow, you have my *best* wishes," said Wensleydale. "But, if it wasn't for this *wretched* lumbago, I'd be marching at the head of my brave troops, wouldn't I Winnie?"

"Yes, Wensleydale," said Winifred, "brave troops."

"Now, let's stop all this nonsense about lumbago," said Parrot. "What I want to know is what do *you* know about rue."

"Rue?" echoed Wensleydale, "rue? What's rue?"

"It's a kind of plant that's supposed to have a good effect on you Weasels," explained Parrot. "Gives you a bit of backbone."

"Hee! hee! hee!" laughed Wensleydale, taking a lace handkerchief from his pocket and fanning himself with it. "You're always *such* a comical bird, Parrot, that saucy wit of yours. Hee! hee! hee! – a plant to give backbone."

"I'll give you wit," said Parrot crossly. "You whimpering, wavering, witless Wensleydale, *listen to me*. Rue is a plant. If you Weasels eat it, it makes you brave and enables you to attack Cockatrices. It's a spell we found in the Great Book of Spells. Now what *I* want to know is whether there's any mention of it in your silly History of Weaseldom."

"How curious," said Wensleydale. "How curious. Rue for making us brave? Not, of course, as you'll appreciate, that we need anything like that. No, of *course* not. Brave as lions, we Weasels, peace-loving of course but when we're roused, har! by Jove, *then* look out!"

"The job is to rouse you," Parrot pointed out. "Now look here, Wensleydale, stop waffling on, there's a good lad. Just let's go and consult your History. You've got it in the library, haven't you?"

"Yes, yes, of course," said Wensleydale. "There's just one thing, though."

"What's that?" asked Parrot.

Wensleydale leant forward and whispered loudly in Parrot's ear. "Can't invite *them* in, those . . . *things* – too big . . . break furniture . . . frighten dear Winnie," he said.

"All right, all right," said Parrot. "If the children go round the back and lie on the lawn they can look through the library window."

"Well, tell them to lie on the lawn *very gently*," said Wensleydale, "that's my croquet lawn."

While Parrot followed Wensleydale and Winifred into the house, the children went round to the back of the house and lay down on the croquet lawn. Peering through the open windows they could see a great oak-panelled library lined with books from floor to ceiling. Presently Wensleydale and Parrot came in.

"Now," said Wensleydale, "the History is over here – shelves Ten, Eleven and Twelve. We have a lot of history, we Weasels, not like *some* creatures one could mention who, strictly speaking, have so little history they might never have existed."

"Let's get on with it," said Parrot. "Has it got an index?"

"Yes," said Wensleydale, pulling out a fat, brown volume. "Here it is."

He took a pair of lorgnettes from his pocket and peered through them, as he opened the Book and started to turn the pages.

"Let's see, now, let's see," he murmured, "rue, rue, rue."

"You're looking under 'X'," said Parrot. "It's spelt R, U, E."

"Of *course*, silly billy, me," said Wensleydale, his nose going pink with embarrassment. "Can't *think* why I thought it started with an 'X'."

"Here it is," said Parrot, triumphantly. "Rue, the use of, for the overpowering of Cockatrices, Page 8424, Volume 95."

"By Jove, who would have thought it," said Wensleydale. "How exciting. My little heart is in a positive *turmoil*, I do assure you. Volume 95 you say, yes – that's shelf 12 – just let me get the ladder."

He got the ladder and climbed up it and extracted the big, fat volume from the shelf, and then he carefully climbed down again and gave the Book to Parrot who spread it out on the table.

"Now, let's see what's what," said Parrot. "Page 8424 – here it is, listen:

'In those days it was discovered by Wormwood
Weasel, the Court Apothecary, that the herb
Rue taken in sufficient quantities made
already stalwart and courageous Weasels
fifty times as brave.
An infusion of this plant taken before battle
ensured victory, especially over Cockatrices,
since, apparently, the Rue made the Weasels'
bite poisonous to them.

However, the Cockatrices, out of vindictive-
ness burnt up the fields of Rue that the
Weasels had cultivated, and since then the
valuable herb has not been obtainable.
And since that day, also, the Cockatrice have
had as their motto "We will rue the day",
meaning that they will be sorry if rue
ever grows in Mythologia again.' "

"Well, bless my periwig and buckles," gasped Wensleydale, "who would have thought it?" He sank into a chair
and fanned himself with his handkerchief. "Fancy *me*,
fifty times as brave as I already *am*! Why, nothing would
stand against me! Why, I'd even go and . . . and . . . and
bite the Chief Cockatrice's leg. What a pity this wonderful, wonderful plant no longer exists. Not for *myself*, you
understand, because I'm brave enough without it, but I
was thinking of my troops. Brave though they are, in
their own way, but in need of something to encourage
them – just a little something."

"If that sentry we saw was an example of your brave
troops, you could do with a little rue," said Parrot.

"Sentry?" asked Wensleydale. "Oh, you mean poor
Wilfred. He's a bag of nerves, that boy, a jangling bag of
nerves. Ever since he found a blue-bottle in his soup, he's
never been the same."

"Well, the point of the thing is *this*," Parrot explained.
"We *know* where to get some rue."

"You do!" cried Wensleydale, excitedly. "Oh, noble
Parrot."

"Now, if we get some, will you and your people drink
it and help us rout the Cockatrices?" asked Parrot.

"Are you quite sure that this rue stuff works?" asked
Wensleydale nervously. "I mean for *your* sakes, dear
Parrot, I wouldn't like to make any promises I couldn't
keep."

"I'm sure it will work," said Parrot. "After all, it's in your own History of Weaseldom."

"Ah yes, history," said Wensleydale, doubtfully. "The trouble with some of these old historians, charming chaps without a doubt but a little bit . . . you know, apt not to be able to tell the difference between *fact* and *fable*. I would simply *love* to help you, dear Parrot, as you know, *honestly* and *truthfully*, nothing, normally, would give me *greater* . . ."

"Listen," interrupted Parrot. "It's our only chance of beating the Cockatrices. If we get the rue will you try it?"

"Well, all right," said Wensleydale, adding hastily, "I won't take it myself, of course, because of my lumbago, but you may try it on one of the under-gardeners."

"Thank goodness for that," said Parrot. "Now you're talking sense."

"When will you bring it?" asked Wensleydale. "I must say I *am* looking forward to this experiment, just *think* how *exciting* if it works. All of us fifty times as brave! My, it makes me come out in weasel pimples just to think of it."

"Yes, well, don't get over-excited," said Parrot. "Got to get the stuff first."

"Now that's where I can be of *positive* help to you, dearest Parrot," said Wensleydale earnestly. "Can I come and help collect it? Perhaps you could cut it while I put it in baskets, or something of the sort?"

"We'd be delighted to have you," said Parrot, "simply delighted. After all, we shall need some help, seeing where the rue grows."

"Where *does* it grow, dear boy?" asked Wensleydale, interested.

"In a clearing in the middle of Mandrake Forest on Werewolf Island," said Parrot grimly.

"Ow! ooh! ow!" yelled Wensleydale, doubling up and clutching himself. "My back, the *agony* of it. Oh, what *torture*, oh, oh, oh." Still screeching, he staggered to the sofa and lay down, putting his lace handkerchief on his brow. "Oh, oh, oh," he moaned. "Oh, my dear Parrot, the *agony*, the *pain*. You see before you a sick and suffering Weasel that's probably not long for this world. Ow! ow! ow! and to think that my lumbago should have got worse just at the moment when I could have been of use to you. Oh, how *shame-making*. Oh, the *pain*. Oh, how *mortified* I am. Oh, the *agony*."

"Oh, be quiet," said Parrot. "I was only pulling your leg. We didn't expect you to come."

"You didn't?" asked Wensleydale, sitting up with his lace handkerchief still on his brow. "You mean you were joking with me? A jest in *very poor taste*, my dear Parrot, if I may say so. To laugh at somebody's lumbago, especially when it's an acute attack, shows a cruel, harsh nature."

"Well, never mind, you'll survive," said Parrot, cheerfully.

"And now, since you're too ill to offer us tea, we'll be off."

"Dear fellow," whispered Wensleydale. "In the normal way I'd be most happy to give you tea, but you've got those big . . . big . . . *things* with you. They'd drink us out of house and home. I can't think why you take them about with you. *What* did you say they were called?"

"Children," said Parrot. "You know, small humans."

"You mean they grow *bigger* than that?" asked Wensleydale, alarmed. "It makes one shudder. I can't see them ever becoming a popular pet, except for people with *very large* houses, of course."

"Well, thanks for your help anyway," said Parrot, and joined the children and Ethelred. They made their way to where the Unicorns awaited them, and remounted.

"Now," said Parrot, as they set off, "we seem to be getting somewhere. We've got the Unicorns' help, which is something, and if this rue works we've got all the Weasels, and that is something. Now, as we're up this way I suggest we drop in on the Griffons. There's only about fifty of them. They're a quiet and industrious colony. If we can get their aid, it will be a great help."

"What exactly are Griffons?" asked Peter.

"Well," said Parrot, "rather nice-looking beasts, I think: lion's body and the head and wings of an eagle; wings of our lot are purely decorative, of course, they can't fly. They used to be purple in the old days, but our lot are a sort of sandy colour. As I say, they're quiet and hard-working, and their chief preoccupation is mining and storing gold. Gold is very important to them; they make their nests out of it, you see. Yes, without gold the Griffons would die out."

"Don't they do anything else?" asked Simon.

"Not really," said Parrot. "They're good, solid chaps, but with practically no sense of humour. You see, when H.H. founded Mythologia the Griffons were practically extinct, and we could find only three pairs in the Swiss Alps. Well, they came here and founded our colony. They run the only gold mine in Mythologia and run it extremely well."

As they had been talking, the Unicorns had been trotting through a narrow gorge filled with a mixture of Bottle and Cork Trees. This now widened out into a spacious, little valley and a strange sight met the children's eyes. On the left-hand side of the valley the cliff-face had a series of tunnels running into it, and these obviously were the mines, for a constant procession of little trucks ran into the tunnels, empty, and reappeared again piled high with great, glittering lumps of gold. The trucks ran to the centre of the valley where there were seven giant cauldrons bubbling and glubbing over fierce fires. As the trucks full of gold arrived at the cauldrons, three Griffons with spades threw the gold lumps into the cauldrons where they were melted down instantly. On the other side three other Griffons scooped up the liquid gold in what looked like long-handled soup ladles and poured it into moulds shaped like bricks. As soon as the gold cooled and hardened, three more Griffons turned out the bricks of gold from the moulds, loaded them into trucks and pushed them into a giant cave that lay on the right-hand side of the valley. This was obviously the important gold store house, the entrance of which was guarded by no less than twelve Griffons that lay on each side of it, as still as statues, only their fierce, golden eyes watching everything carefully.

As soon as one of the sentries saw the little cavalcade of Unicorns, he sat up on his hind legs and spread his wings and blew a series of three blasts from a slender, golden trumpet. Immediately, all the Griffons stopped whatever they were doing and gathered round, and yet more Griffons, covered and sparkling with gold dust, appeared from the mine shafts and soon the children were surrounded by some fifty Griffons. They were inclined to agree with Parrot's description of them as being nice-looking beasts. Each was the size of a very large dog, with the body of a lion and a lion's tawny coat. Their huge, eagle heads – though fierce-looking with a strong, curved beak – had a kindly expression in the large, keen eyes. Their wings they would occasionally spread above their heads and stretch and flap them as hawks do.

"Good morning, good morning gold digger Griffons," said Parrot when they were all assembled. "I bring you greetings from H.H."

The Griffons all said, "Good morning," in growly, deep voices like lions.

And then they pushed one of their number forward as spokesman. "Ve are much pleased to see you, Herr Parrot," he said in his rich voice.

"Ja, ja," chorused the rest of the Griffons, nodding their heads.

"Ve have heard that the Cockatrices have killed you

and H.H. both, so ve vere much sad," the Griffon went on.

"Well, both I, as you can see, and H.H., are very well indeed," said Parrot. "It's just that the Cockatrices have suddenly become disobedient."

"That is very bad," said the Griffon. "Cockatrices should not disobedient be."

"Yes," Parrot went on. "They've stolen the Great Books of Government and are holding them in Cockatrice Castle, and we plan to get them – me and these kind children here."

"Any friend of Herr Parrot is a friend of the Griffons," said the Griffon inclining his head.

"The Cockatrices need a good lesson," said Parrot. "We can't have them running the country. Already they're producing an egg a day. Who knows where it will end? The next thing is that they'll be banning gold as a nest building material."

"Vat?" roared all the Griffons. "Dis ve vould not allow."

"Well, there you are," said Parrot. "That's the sort of thing we're trying to put a stop to. We've got the Unicorns and the Toads on our side, as well as the Weasels, and we want to know if we can count on your help?"

The Griffons conferred together, talking to each other in their deep, rumbling voices with much swishing of wings and clattering of beaks. At last the spokesman said to Parrot: "Ve are agreed. Ve vill join you. Ve t'ink Government by dese Cockatrice vill be bad t'ing for Mythologia. Ve your instructions vill avait."

"Thank you," said Parrot. "We will send a message to you when we're ready."

"At your service alvays," said the Griffon bowing.

As the children rode out of the valley, they could hear the clink, clink, clink of the Griffons' hammers hammering away deep in the mines and the bubbling and plopping noise of the liquid gold boiling in the great cauldrons.

"That's marvellous," said Peter, enthusiastically, as they left the valley. "I like the Griffons, just the sort of people one would like to have around in a tight corner."

"They're slow but sure," said Parrot.

"Well, now we're collecting something like an army," said Simon, "with the Unicorns, the Weasels and the Griffons. We've got nearly a thousand people."

"And we'll need it," said Parrot. "Those Cockatrices won't give in easily. Their castle is practically impregnable."

"Wot does impregnable mean?" asked Ethelred, jogging up and down behind Penelope on her Unicorn.

"It means you can't get into it easily," Penelope explained.

"Ho, can't you just?" said Ethelred. "Wot about that drain wot I showed you?"

"They'll have found that by now and filled it in, I'm afraid," said Parrot.

"Well, wot I say is this," said Ethelred. "I'm not such a useless Toad as some people might think, and I've played about in that Castle, Toad and Tadpole, for years now. Wot I don't know about that there Castle isn't worth knowing, and I say it's not as impregers ... impregers ... as wot you said."

"Well, we'll see," said Parrot. "When we come to plan the final campaign, your knowledge will be of the utmost value to us."

They were riding through very dense Cork forest when suddenly the Unicorns, who had been trotting along quite happily, stopped and started to rear and mill around.

"Hey! hey! hey!" said Parrot. "What's the to-do?"

But the two Unicorns carrying Simon and Peter with Parrot on his shoulder, bolted off into the forest. Penelope's Unicorn reared on to its hind legs, throwing Penelope and Ethelred off its back, before it also galloped off into the forest. Penelope fell into the bushes with a bump that knocked all the breath out of her body, and Ethelred, still clasping Penelope's Red-Cross bag, fell on his head in the middle of the path and lay stunned. Penelope was just about to get up and go to him, to see if he was badly hurt, when her blood froze. Around the corner of the path, out of the Cork forest, appeared three Cockatrices; their scales were rattling as they marched, their pale eyes glaring. Penelope sank back into the bushes and stayed quite still, hoping that the Cockatrices wouldn't notice Ethelred, but since he was lying right in the middle of the path this was a vain hope. He was just sitting up and rubbing his head and groaning when the Cockatrices came up to him.

"Har," said the leading Cockatrice in a nasty, gobbling voice. "What have we here?"

"I'm a Peruvian greengrocer, wot's 'ere travelling around to collect a cargo of Moon-carrots," said Ethelred immediately, and with great confidence.

"You don't look like a Peruvian greengrocer," said the Cockatrice, peering at him, little wisps of flame and smoke trailing from his nostrils. "You look more like a Toad."

"Well, I'll let you into a secret" said Ethelred, smiling up at the Cockatrice. "But, at first, would you mind moving your beak a little bit? I don't want to get me 'at singed."

"Well," said the Cockatrice, standing back. "What's the secret?"

"Well," said Ethelred. "I'm a Toad – that's quite true. I'm disguised as a Peruvian greengrocer because I'm incognito."

"What?" snarled the Cockatrice.

"I'm in disguise," Ethelred explained.

"Why?" asked the Cockatrice.

"Because," said Ethelred, "I'm on a very important mission, that's why. I'm carrying a very valuable present 'ere from the 'ead Griffon to the Chief Cockatrice."

"What is the present?" asked the Cockatrice.

"It's a Complete Master Spy's outfit," said Ethelred, patting the Red-Cross bag. "In 'ere is the equipment that will turn you into an Australian sheep farmer on vacation or a Lithuanian ambassador to Togoland, in a flash."

"I don't believe you, Toad," snarled the Cockatrice. "Show me what you have in the bag."

Penelope held her breath, for she knew that all the things in the bag were medical supplies she had brought. She felt sure that Ethelred was doomed, for when the Cockatrices saw what was in the bag they would surely arrest Ethelred, if they did no worse.

" 'Ere, I can't do that," Ethelred protested. "It's not good manners to show you other people's presents."

"If you don't show me, I shall arrest you," said the Cockatrice. " 'Ere," said Ethelred, playing for time. "You've got no right to arrest me. Wot 'ave I done?"

"We are the Government. Therefore we have every right to arrest you," said the Cockatrice. "At your execution, your crime will be read out for you to hear. Open the bag."

"Oh, all right then," said Ethelred, sulkily. He opened the bag and emptied the contents on to the ground, while the three Cockatrices bent over it interestedly, peering with their pale straw-coloured eyes.

"What's that?' asked one Cockatrice, pointing at a roll of cotton-wool?"

"False 'air," said Ethelred immediately. "Stick it on your 'ead and you're an old man of ninety in a second."

"And that?" asked the second Cockatrice, pointing at the bandages.

"Bandages," said Ethelred. "Wrap 'em round you and you're a wounded warrior in a trice. Wrap 'em round your 'ead and your own mum wouldn't know you."

"And this?" asked the third Cockatrice, pointing at a bottle of iodine.

"'Indu make-up," said Ethelred airily. "Splash it on your face, couple of bandages round your 'ead, a ruby or two, and you're a maharajah wot's so lifelike you could deceive an elephant."

"And this?" asked the Head Cockatrice, pointing to a small bottle.

This bottle, Penelope knew, contained lavender-water which she'd brought because it was cooling and soothing if somebody had a headache or sunstroke.

"Invisible ink," said Ethelred.

"But why isn't it invisible?" asked the Cockatrice.

"Because invisible ink *isn't*," Ethelred explained. "It's wot it *writes* wot's invisible, not the ink."

"I don't believe you," said the Cockatrice. "Open the bottle and let me see you write something invisible."

"You ain't 'alf a disbelieving lot," grumbled Ethelred. "How can you see me write something wot's invisible?"

Nevertheless, he picked up the bottle and uncorked it, and immediately the most extraordinary thing happened. The three Cockatrices reeled back, the tears streaming from their eyes and they started sneezing. As they sneezed, great gushes of flame and smoke shot from their nostrils, and Ethelred, holding the bottle of lavender-water with one hand and his top hat on with the other, had to hop to and fro with great agility to prevent himself from being burnt.

"Why," thought Penelope to herself, "they're behaving just like the one that was chasing Septimus; it must have been lavender-water it could smell. I must have had some on my clothes."

Suddenly the three Cockatrices could stand it no longer. Wheezing and gasping for breath, their eyes watering, sneezing great sheets of flame, they turned and ran, coughing and spluttering into the Cork forest.

"Cor blimey," said Ethelred, gazing after them in astonishment. "Suffering frog's spawn. 'Ood 'ave thought it?"

"Ethelred," said Penelope, coming out of the bushes, some of which were still smouldering, "that was the bravest thing I've ever seen anyone do."

"Cor, miss, it wasn't nuffink," said Ethelred, going a deep crimson.

"Not only were you brave, but you discovered something the Cockatrices don't like, and that'll be a great help to us in our battle," said Penelope.

"You mean the lavender-water, miss?" asked Ethelred. "Yes, that did seem to get them in a pickle, I must admit."

"I'm not quite sure how we can use it," said Penelope, "but I'm sure one of the others will be able to think of a way."

Just at that moment Peter and Simon appeared, galloping back through the woods with Penelope's Unicorn following behind.

"Are you all right, Penny?" shouted Simon.

"Quite all right," she shouted back.

"It was these stupid Unicorns," shouted Peter. "They said they could smell Cockatrice . . ." His voice died away as he saw all the smouldering bushes, charred trees. "So the Unicorns were right," he said, "there were Cockatrices about."

"And if it hadn't been for Ethelred's bravery, I don't know *what* would have happened," said Penelope, climbing on to her Unicorn.

"'Ere steady on, miss," said Ethelred, as he took his place behind her. "You're making me all embarrassed."

"Ethelred's made a most important discovery," said

Penelope. "But with all these Cockatrices about, it's not safe here. Let's get back to the Crystal Caves and I'll tell you about it there."

"Come on, then," said Parrot, "full steam ahead."

And at a smart canter they headed for the Crystal Caves

six

THE SINGING SEA

When they got back to the Caves, H.H. was terribly excited at the news that the Weasels *might* join, that the Griffons *would* join, and that Ethelred had found something that threw Cockatrices into convulsions.

"Lavender-water?" he said. "How interesting. It gives them a form of hay fever, I expect, like having a very nasty cold. I wonder if I can make up a substitute?"

"Don't you grow lavender here?" asked Penelope.

"It grows on one of the islands," said H.H., "but without Hepsibar's Herbal I'm afraid I can't remember which one."

"I got terrible hay fever once from a plant when I went on holiday," said Tabitha. "Let me just smell it and see if it's the same."

So they gave her the lavender-water to smell, and it had the same effect that it had on the Cockatrice, and Tabitha set fire to two sofas, fourteen cushions and a table with her sneezes, before she was brought back to normal by a bucket of water being poured over her head.

"That's it, that was the plant," she gasped. "Oh my goodness me, I haven't sneezed like that since I used pepper in mistake for face powder."

"Why on earth did you do that?" asked Penelope in surprise.

"Well, I was making up in the dark, you see," she explained, wiping her still streaming eyes.

"Making up in the dark?" said Penelope. "Whatever for?"

"Well, it was a midnight ball that I was going to. There was no moon, you see, so naturally you make up in the dark," said Tabitha.

Penelope was so confused by this that she gave up the subject altogether.

"Where did you say this plant grew?" asked H.H.

"Golden Goose Island," said Tabitha. "Us dragons went on a camping holiday there. We all got it. You can imagine how it spoilt our holiday."

Having seen the damage that one Dragon could do, suffering from hay (or should it be lavender) fever, the children could imagine the turmoil of fifty camping Dragons all having lavender fever at the same time.

"Well that *is* useful," said H.H. in a pleased tone of voice. "Golden Goose Island lies on the direct route to Werewolf Island, so you can gather some lavender on your way back. I'll then make up an infusion of it and we'll keep it handy."

"Now we'd better plan the voyage," said Simon. "Have you got a chart, H.H.?"

"Yes, I have an excellent one," said H.H. and he pulled out a great parchment map which showed the whole of Mythologia and the sea and all its islands. "Now we are *here*," said H.H., adjusting his glasses, "and there is Cockatrice Castle over there. Now you'll have to get down here, to the beach, and head in the south-westerly direction, past Moonraker's Marsh, past the Agate Archipelago, then you'll see Golden Goose Island on your left, and north-north-east of that lies Werewolf Island."

"How long do you think the voyage will take us?" asked Peter.

"Oh, several hours," said H.H.

"I suppose you haven't got such a thing as an outboard engine, have you?" asked Simon hopefully.

"I'm afraid not," said H.H. "But we can make you a

Moon-calf jelly sail and I'll give you a spanking wind to help you along. How's that?"

"Splendid," said Peter. "You know, next to attacking Cockatrice Castle, this seems to be an *excellent* adventure."

"Don't speak too soon," warned Parrot. "Those Werewolves are nasty customers."

"*You're* not going," screamed Dulcibelle, suddenly. "You're not going to Werewolf Island, I won't have it. I shall sulk. I shall resign. I shall go into hibernation. I shall scream. I shall shout; I shall never ever never ever speak to you again, so there."

So saying, she burst into tears and pulled down all the curtains on her cage.

Penelope went across to Parrot's cage to talk to her.

"Dulcibelle dear," she said, "we know you think the world of Parrot – and so do we – so we wouldn't ask him to come unless it was absolutely necessary, you must realise that. But I promise you that if you let him come, I will see that he takes no risks and leaves all the dangerous work to my cousins and me."

"Well," said Dulcibelle, raising one curtain and wiping her eyes with the corner of it. "If you promise to look after him."

"I promise," said Penelope.

"Now if you women have finished," said Parrot in a loud and embarrassed voice, "perhaps we can get on with the planning of this mission."

"I reckon," said Simon who had been doing a lot of mathematics on a piece of paper, during all this, "I reckon that if H.H. gives us a four-knot wind at dawn tomorrow, barring accidents, we should reach Werewolf Island by three-thirty in the afternoon. That means that we can collect the rue and sail all night and be back here at dawn the day after."

"Do you think you can do it in that time?" asked H.H.,

doubtfully. "On no account must you land at night. That's when the Werewolves are most dangerous."

"If you can give us a steady wind," said Simon, "we should do it."

"That's no trouble," said H.H. "You just tell me the direction and the force and I'll turn it on – nothing simpler."

"You must take your sea-sick pills," shouted Dulcibelle, suddenly.

"Do be quiet, woman," said Parrot crossly. "We're discussing important things."

"Sea-sickness is important," said Dulcibelle. "If you're so sea-sick you can't run away from a Werewolf – *that's* important."

"I promise I'll see that he takes them," said Penelope soothingly.

"I'd love to come with you," said Tabitha, "and help, but I'm afraid I'm too big for the boat."

"You're too big and I'm too old," said H.H. "Ah well, but I feel guilty at letting you children do all the work and take all the risks."

"Nonsense," said Peter. "I wouldn't have missed this for the world."

"Nor would I," said Simon.

"You're not to worry," said Penelope, throwing her arms around H.H. and kissing him on his rosy cheek. "We love helping you and we'll get Mythologia back for you, you see if we don't."

" 'Ere, 'ere, three cheers for Miss Penelope," said Ethelred, clapping.

"You're very kind, very kind," said H.H., taking off his glasses which had suddenly become misty, and blowing his nose violently.

"Miss," Ethelred said eagerly. "Can I come too, miss? I'm not very big like and I wouldn't take up much room, and I might be able to 'elp."

"Of course, he can come," said Simon, "brave Toad."

"Yes, of course," agreed Peter, "quick-witted Ethelred."

"You can come as my personal protector," said Penelope, "and we'll be proud to have you with us."

Ethelred was so overcome that he went as red as fourteen pounds of over-ripe tomatoes, and he had to go into a corner and blow *his* nose very vigorously several times.

So the next morning, having said goodbye to H.H., Tabitha and a most tearful Dulcibelle, the children with Parrot and Ethelred went down one of the many corridors in the Crystal Caves which eventually led them out on the beach, where the sand was like minute pearls and the tiny champagne-coloured waves broke on the shore with a musical noise like somebody running their fingers along the strings of the most melodious of harps. No wonder, Penelope thought, it was called the 'Singing Sea'. So into this gentle and melodious sea they launched the dinghy, and immediately as H.H. had promised a warm breeze sprang up, the sail furled out like a bay window, and the dinghy went bowling along at a good rate, carrying with it Penelope, the boys, Parrot and Ethelred, and a hamper full of food provided by H.H. They also had sickles for cutting the rue and the lavender and large bags for putting it in.

"Tell me, Parrot," said Penelope, and felt that she had been asking the same question ever since they'd arrived in Mythologia, "what are Werewolves exactly? I'm sure I've read about them but I can't quite remember."

"I remember," said Simon, "weren't they people who were supposed to turn into wolves at full moon?"

"That's right," said Parrot, "an ugly superstition, as well as being a silly one. But, as I told you, in the days when H.H. created Mythologia a lot of people believed firmly in Werewolves and so there were quite a number about. They begged to be allowed to come to Mythologia, as they began to die out, and H.H. had to let them. They were a borderline case, of course, but he gave them the benefit of the doubt. He let them set up house on this Island we are going to, on condition that they shared it with the two other trouble-makers, the Mandrakes and the Will-o-the-Wisps. Then the Firedrakes wanted a fairly gloomy sort of island, so he let them live there too."

"I've heard of the Will-o-the-Wisps and how they lead you into swamps and quicksands," said Penelope, "but what are Firedrakes?"

"Very colourful," said Parrot. "The most colourful thing in Mythologia, related to the Will-o-the-Wisps, but they can be hot and cold, whereas the Wisps are only cold, of course. Firedrakes are nice little fellows, very timid, but with charming, straightforward characters. The Will-o-the-Wisps, on the other hand, are an unruly lot, mischievous and troublemakers."

"And the Mandrakes?" asked Penelope. "Are they something like Firedrakes?"

"No, no," said Parrot. "Firedrakes are composed mainly of fire, but the Mandrakes are plants – lazy, good-for-nothing plants at that. You see, at one time they were widely used in spells and medicine, and of course they didn't like that, so they invented the scream."

"The *scream*?" said Peter. "How do you invent a scream, for goodness' sake?"

"It's such a terrible scream," said Parrot, holding up a claw to emphasise his words, "such a hideous, horrifying scream that when you hear it it drives you mad."

"This was to prevent them from getting plucked?" asked Simon.

"Yes," said Parrot, "so now they do nothing but sleep day and night, night and day, and should anyone be silly enough to wake them then they all wake up at once and scream at once – and you can imagine what that's like."

"Gosh, and we've got to get through a wood of those?" asked Peter. "It is going to be dangerous."

"I told you this mission is going to be dangerous," said Parrot. "First we have the Mandrakes to worry about, then the Werewolves, and the Will-o-the-Wisps, though they won't be about in the day-time and the Wolves will be asleep too. That's why H.H. insisted that we only landed on the Island during the day. It's the least dangerous time."

"We're making good progress, owing to H.H.'s wind," said Simon.

Indeed, the dinghy was bowling over the musical, champagne-coloured waves at a good pace. What with the warm sun and warm wind it was a delightful journey. The water was so clear that twenty feet below them the children could see schools of multi-coloured fish swimming about, huge oysters with pearls gleaming in them and giant lobsters and crabs in a variety of colours. Little flocks of scarlet and blue flying fish would suddenly appear in front of their bows, fly along the surface for a little way, chittering like birds, before plunging into the sea again.

"'Ere miss," said Ethelred in a low voice to Penelope, "you're not afraid of them Werewolves, are you? There's no need to be, with me along to look after you, 'onest."

"I should have been scared," Penelope said, "but with you as my personal protector I don't feel the slightest cause for alarm."

Ethelred looked immensely pleased at this.

They had been travelling for several hours and the soothing wind and sun had made them all tired. Parrot put his head under his wing for forty winks; Ethelred lay on his back with his mouth open, snoring, his top hat on his chest; and Penelope and the boys dozed in the balmy air. After Penelope had slept for a while, she woke and lay there thinking that perhaps they all ought to have some lunch, and staring up at the clear, green sky with little battalions of coloured clouds, she suddenly felt that there was something wrong, but she couldn't think what it could be. Then she realised what it was. They were not moving. She sat up and looked round. As far as she could see in every direction they were surrounded by great fronds of seaweed, like purple and green lace, that was actually moving and growing as she watched. The dinghy was, of course, firmly aground on the fronds, and that's why they were not moving. Then Penelope suddenly realised the danger they were in, for a frond of the beautiful seaweed made its way over the side of the dinghy, like the tentacle of an animal, but growing and expanding as it moved with a faint rustling sound. Penelope realised that they only had to have two or three bits like this and the dinghy and they themselves would disappear under the pile of purple and green seaweed.

"Parrot," she shouted, struggling to open the hamper in which she knew there was a knife to cut the seaweed. "Parrot . . . everyone . . . wake up, wake up."

They all woke up and saw in an instant what the problem was.

"Oh cumbersome and cumulus cauliflowers," exclaimed Parrot in annoyance. "It's that wretched weed. I'd forgotten about it. Here, just cut off the bits that come aboard. It will soon stop."

Sure enough, after the children and Ethelred had cut off two or three fronds of the seaweed, it seemed to realise that it was not wanted and ceased trying to grow all over the dinghy. But they continued to remain stationary.

"A dreadful nuisance this," said Parrot. "This wretched weed will hold us up unless I can find Desdemona. Here, give me my telescope, Penelope, will you, it's just beside you."

With his telescope, Parrot anxiously scanned the horizon until suddenly he gave a squawk of satisfaction.

"We're in luck," he said, "they're working over there. The thing is to attract their attention."

"Who are they?" asked Penelope.

"Mermaids," said Parrot. "H.H. employs them to keep the weeds under control. You see, he made a mistake with the spell. Instead of being everlasting, you know like the flowers you saw, he said ever-growing. And once you've gone and done a spell like that, it's impossible to undo, so he had to get the Mermaids just to keep it down. It's a full-time job I can tell you. If they relax for a moment the Singing Sea would be full of it. I think what we'll have to do is to pull ourselves a little nearer and shout."

So they all leant over the side and grabbed armfuls of weeds and pulled. Slowly, inch by inch, they found they could slide the dinghy over the weeds. After pulling and panting for what seemed an age, the children could hear a faint singing drifting across the weeds and water.

"Ahoy," roared Parrot, "ahoy there, Desdemona, ahoy."

The singing ceased and there was silence.

"Ahoy," roared Parrot again, "it's me, Parrot."

Still there was silence. Then, suddenly, right next to the dinghy the weeds parted and an enormous Mermaid made her appearance, slightly out of breath. She did not look at all like Penelope's idea of a mermaid, for she must have weighed easily twenty stone. She had vast quantities of bright blonde hair that fell all over her shoulders and chest in ringlets. Her eyes, which were large, circular and bright periwinkle blue, had vast quantities of eye-shadow on the lids and black false eyelashes, so long and thick that they were more like hedges. Her plump hands were beautifully manicured, the nails painted a bright cyclamen pink, and in one of them she held a golden sickle and in the other a large silver mirror.

"Did I hear a man calling for help?" she inquired in a

deep, husky voice, fluttering her eyelashes so hard that Penelope thought that they might fall off. "A man, no doubt, of blue blood and ancient lineage, calling upon me for succour?"

"No," said Parrot, "it was me. How are you, Des?"

"Oh," said Desdemona coldly. "Oh, it's *you* Parrot. How simply ripping it is to see you again. I do wish, by the way, that you would not refer to me in that coarse, vulgar way as Des. My name is Desdemona and I'll thank you to use it."

"Right'o," said Parrot. "Let me introduce you – Penelope, Peter, Simon – Miss Desdemona Williamson Smythe-Smythe-Browne, Head Mermaid."

The mermaid laid her massive arms on the side of the dinghy, causing it to tip up at a dangerous angle, and shook hands graciously with each of the children in turn.

"Charmed to meet you, I'm sure," said Desdemona, fluttering her eyelids. "Such handsome boys and *such* a pretty girl. No tails of course, but don't let that worry you, it's not *your* fault. I expect you all have blue blood in your veins, don't you with names like those?"

"I don't think so," said Penelope. "I think ours is red."

"Pity," said Desdemona, "but we can't *all* have blue blood. I expect you're terribly well connected with all sorts of dukes and duchesses and lords in your family, without a doubt, I'm sure. I can see it in your faces, aristocrats, that's what."

"No, I don't think even that," said Penelope regretfully.

"Oh, I am sure they're there if you search for them," said Desdemona. "Take me, for example. Well, I mean to say, you can tell I am well-connected, can't you? It's something to do with the bearing – majestic that's what. But, I mean to say, one doesn't like to mention those things for fear of being thought a snob. No, just one's natural, aristocratic bearing tells people you're – well, you know, a cut above them."

"Exactly," said Penelope, trying not to smile.

"My whole family is well-connected," said Desdemona, "on both sides. Oh yes, ever so well connected. Do you know, one of my aunts by marriage was waved at by Christopher Columbus? My father's uncle's sister's cousin, she, for many years I am told, received letters from no less a person than Lord Nelson hisself – letters of the most loving nature."

"Really," said Penelope.

"Yes," said Desdemona, earnestly. "And then there was my uncle's mother's brother, you know – not the one that had his back scraped to *ribbons* by the Armada – well, he . . ."

"Look Des," said Parrot impatiently. "Can't we leave your family history alone until some other time?"

"My dear Parrot," said Desdemona with dignity. "I am sorry, I'm sure, if I'm boring you with accounts of my good connections. It's very seldom I get the chance to talk to people of culture and refinement, as you well know, and I am sure that *they* are interested, and even if they *weren't* they're far too *well-bred* to say so, unlike you, what's behaving as common as dirt."

"Why, I don't mind hearing about your family," said Parrot cheerfully. "It's just that we're in an awful hurry and this weed's slowing us down. Could you get some of your wenches to cut us a path and give us a push? It's a matter of life and death, old girl, otherwise we wouldn't worry you."

"Well," said Desdemona, "seeing as how it's an emergency, I will certainly ask my *young ladies* if they would assist you in your predicament. However, I would be glad if you would call me by my correct name and not 'old girl' in that disgustingly familiar fashion. We Mermaids of good connection can't be too careful about our good names, and the use of that expression might lead people to suppose that you and I were on more friendly terms than what we are."

"All right, Miss Williamson-Smythe-Smythe-Browne," said Parrot, in exasperation. "Anything you like, but just get a rescue party."

"Common as common some of them round here," said Desdemona in a low voice to Penelope. "Not like you and me." She gave Peter and Simon a sparkling smile, waved a fat hand and sank back into the weed bed and disappeared with scarcely a ripple.

"Drat this delay," said Parrot irritably, pulling his watch out from under his wing and looking at it. "We're three hours behind. That means we'll really have to get a move on when we get out of this weed. We never allowed for anything like *this* in our plan."

Quite soon Desdemona surfaced again by the dinghy and with her emerged eight Mermaids of much the same age and shape. Some had yellow hair like Desdemona's, others had scarlet hair, and some, whose hair was obviously white, had dyed it an electric blue.

"Young ladies," said Desdemona, in her rich husky voice, "I know you will agree that it is a very great honour to have here with us people what are as well connected as what we are. I'm sure I speak for you all when I say welcome to the cultured and aristocratic company of Lady Penelope and her cousins what are lords and such in their own right."

" 'Ere," said Ethelred suddenly, "wot about me then?"

"You, what about you?" asked Desdemona.

"Well, I'm a Polish count, I am," said Ethelred, "and come from a long and distinguished line of counts I do."

"You?" said Desdemona in astonishment. "You don't *look* like a count."

"Corse I don't," said Ethelred. "I was changed in me cradle, wasn't I, see?"

"Forgive me," said Desdemona, "but you don't *talk* like a count."

"That's because I was rescued by this little, old lady wot brought me up as 'er son," said Ethelred. "She didn't 'ave no money, see, so she couldn't heducate me to talk proper."

"Fascinating, quite fascinating," said Desdemona, doubtfully. "You must tell me all about it. But first, young ladies, let us rescue our noble cargo. Now, all together: heave-o, and away we go."

Displaying much more agility than one would have thought possible from Mermaids of such ample figures, Desdemona's eight young ladies started scything a path through the weeds, while Desdemona herself swam to the stern and leant her fat arms on it, while propelling the dinghy with her tail, and settled down for a good gossip.

"When I was a gal," she confided to Penelope, "before we came and settled in Mythologia, I used to spend a *lot* of my time in the sea off Brighton."

"Brighton?" said Peter, "Simon and I spent our summer holidays there last year."

"Did you?" said Desdemona. "Lovely place. Always got such a nice class of person there, if you know what I mean. You know, my aunt, on my father's side that is, she was swimming there one day, and you'll never *guess* who came out of one of those bathing machines."

"Who?" asked Simon.

"King George the Fourth," said Desdemona. "Oh yes, His Royal Highness hisself. All dressed up in a lovely striped bathing suit he was, my aunt said, and wearing a woolly hat to keep his Royal head dry, bless him; and he was wearing beach shoes on his Royal feet, so that they wouldn't get cut on the stones. Well, he'd hardly got up to his waist in water when he lost one of his shoes. Such goings on as you'd never believe, my aunt said. King

George shouting and roaring, and all the courtiers and equerries in their land clothes diving like mad things to find the shoe."

"And what happened?" asked the children fascinated.

"They didn't find it," said Desdemona. "But when they'd all gone, my aunt went and had a look, and *she* found it. Yes, and she's got it to this very day in a little glass case – the very beach shoe what was on his Royal Highness's foot. What do you think of *that*?"

"There can't be many people whose aunts have royal beach shoes," said Penelope.

"Exactly," said Desdemona in triumph. "That's what I'm always telling my girls. Do you go to many garden parties at Buckingham Palace, my dear?"

"No, not often," said Penelope truthfully.

"My grandmother swam up the Thames once and was run down by a barge. At first, she was very annoyed, for it gave her a black eye, and then she realised that it was Queen Elizabeth's own state barge. Just fancy that! Not many people can say they've been given a black eye by a Queen, now can they?"

"Clear sea ahead," shouted Parrot. "Get ready to hoist the sail."

"Well, I have enjoyed our little chat," said Desdemona graciously. "There's nothing like a bit of chin-wag with one what knows what you're talking about when you mention the aristocracy."

"I've enjoyed it too," said Penelope.

"I hope we meet again," said Simon.

"Yes, I hope so too," said Peter.

"You're all very gracious," said Desdemona, fluttering her eyelashes like mad.

She gathered her ladies about her and they all bobbed about in the water, throwing kisses and waving, as the dinghy gathered speed and drew away across the sea.

"Most *vexatious* delay," said Parrot, worriedly consulting

his watch. "Most *vexatious*. And it doesn't seem that we shall go any faster. This means that we won't get to Werewolf Island before dark."

"But H.H. said not to go ashore after dark," protested Peter.

"I don't think we have any choice," said Parrot, grimly. "If we don't go ashore and get the rue tonight, we'll miss the wind H.H. is putting up for us, and it'll take *days* to get back."

"Well, then it's up to Peter, you and me," said Simon. "Penny can stay with the dinghy, and Ethelred will stay with her to guard her."

"*Now*, look," Penelope began.

"Please, Penelope," said Parrot. "Simon is quite right. If it was daytime it would be different, but at night it's far too dangerous. We simply can't trust the Werewolves or the Will-o-the-Wisps, to say nothing of the Mandrakes. You must stay with the dinghy, like a good girl, and you and Ethelred can push off into deep water if anything happens."

"Oh, all right," said Penelope. "But I don't want to."

The dinghy sped on over the waves, and Parrot became more and more worried, looking at his watch every five minutes and scanning the horizon through his telescope. He was just doing this for the fiftieth time when a strange thing happened. Just ahead of them the sea suddenly boiled and frothed, as if there were a sandbank or a reef that had suddenly appeared. The waves got rougher and rougher in that one spot. And then the children, who were somewhat alarmed, could see something rising to the surface of the sea. The next moment the huge head of a Sea Serpent broke surface and rose some thirty feet in the air on a long slender neck. It was an enormous head, with nostrils like a Hippo's, huge saucer-like eyes, tattered-looking ears so large that, at first, the children thought they were wings. Around its chin and lips were a lot of bristly tentacles that made it look as though it had a beard and moustache. Its body was covered with the most beautiful kingfisher blue scales, its eyes were sea-green and its beard and moustache were bright ginger. It had two strange, black horns on the top of its head between its ears that looked rather like a snail's horns, and, behind them, it wore a chef's hat. It peered about it, smiling to itself, the sea running off it in waterfalls.

Far from being alarmed at this apparition, Parrot seemed positively delighted. "Oh *good*," he said. "It's Oswald. What a bit of luck."

"Is he friendly?" asked Penelope.

Of all the animals they'd seen in Mythologia, Oswald was undoubtedly the biggest.

"Oswald?" said Parrot. "Oswald? Har! har! har! Tamest creature in Mythologia."

"It was just that he seems to have an awful lot of teeth," explained Penelope.

"No, Oswald's all right," said Parrot. "Tame as three sheep is Oswald."

"Will he help us?" asked Simon.

"That's what I'm going to ask him," said Parrot. "The thing is to attract his attention – he's a bit hard of hearing."

So saying, Parrot went up into the bows of the dinghy, cupped his wings round his beak and shouted: "Oswald. It's me, Parrot. I'm here, you ninny, in the boat."

Oswald looked vaguely about, as though he had heard some sound but couldn't place it. Then suddenly he saw the dinghy. Immediately, his eyes widened in astonishment. "A crumpet!" he screamed with delight. "After all these years – a crumpet, a blue crumpet!"

He surged forward, this creature that Parrot had said was the tamest in Mythologia, bent down, and before anyone could do anything sensible he had engulfed in his mouth the dinghy, the three children, Parrot, Ethelred, the hamper full of food, the sickles and the bag for the rue.

"Oh dear," thought Penelope, as the huge jaws, with their white teeth, closed round them. "This *definitely* is the end of our adventure."

✕

seven

WEREWOLVES AND FIREDRAKES

"Oh, the ninny," shouted Parrot in the gloom of Oswald's mouth. "Oh, the stupid nincompoop. Really these creatures are enough to make one moult."

"What are we going to do?" asked Peter.

"Do?" shouted Parrot. "*Do?* Get out of here before that idiot Sea Serpent swallows us. Here, you take the sickles and give me my telescope, and we'll bang on his teeth."

"Yum yum," they heard Oswald say to himself, his voice sounding all hollow and echoing from where they were. "Yum yum. After all these years, what a delicious flavour! So delicately made! Yum yum. A *real* crumpet at last."

"I'll give the silly fool crumpet," said Parrot. "Now, all together."

So, just as Oswald was saying "Yum yum" for the fourth time, the children, Ethelred and Parrot, all hit his teeth at the same time. So what he actually said was, "Yum yum, ooer ouch, ahh," and, without more ado, spat out the dinghy and its contents.

Then he put his head down and stared at it. "Why?" he said in astonishment, "it's a crumpet with *people* on. Well, I never."

"It's me, you idiot. Parrot," shouted Parrot, waving his telescope.

"Now, a white crumpet with people on would be extraordinary enough," said Oswald, fascinated by this problem, "but a blue crumpet with people on it is, I am sure, something no one has seen before."

"I'll half-strangle this reptile before I've finished," muttered Parrot, then he shouted, "*Oswald, it's me, Parrot, Parrot.*"

Oswald peered closely into the dinghy. "Why," he said in pleased surprise. "It's Parrot, I do believe. How nice to see you. But what are you doing sailing about in a blue crumpet? Very dangerous, you know, my dear fellow, you might get eaten by someone. Then where would you be? If you must sail about, do it properly in a galleon or something of the sort."

"This is not a crumpet, it's a boat," roared Parrot.

"Goat?" said Oswald. "No, no, my dear Parrot. I hate to contradict you, but I saw a goat once and it looked nothing like that, besides goats don't float and they're not blue. No, no, mark my words – it's a crumpet. One of them blue marzipan ones they make in Bulgaria."

"I can't talk to you without your ear trumpet," shouted Parrot. "I'm getting hoarse."

"No," said Oswald, "it's not a horse either. I mean, I *may* be mistaken. It could, I suppose, be a blue muffin, but I doubt it; I very much doubt it. I don't think a muffin would float so well."

"What's the use of having the largest ears in Mythologia, if you can't hear," said Parrot in exasperation, and then flew up and perched on Oswald's ear.

"Where's your *trumpet*?" he yelled.

"Ahh," said Oswald, pleased. "I thought it was, I'm glad you agree, dear Parrot. A goat is something *quite* different – with horns and a tail and things."

"Your ear trumpet," yelled Parrot. "*Trumpet, trumpet, trumpet.*"

"No need to shout and yell like that," said Oswald, hurt. "I can hear perfectly well without your screeching and roaring."

"Your *ear trumpet*," shouted the children in unison.

"Oh, you'd like to see it?" said Oswald, pleased. "Just

a moment, I've got it here – the very latest thing. Of course, I don't really need it. I can hear perfectly well, but it's a comfort to have it around, and I find that if you pour icing sugar through it, it makes the most delicious patterns on cakes."

He fumbled under the waves and then one of his scaly paws appeared, holding a huge, amber ear trumpet, decorated in silver.

He pressed it into his ear and beamed at them.

"How does it look?" he inquired. "Rather saucy, I thought."

"Beautiful," shouted the children.

"Eh?" said Oswald, bending down and putting the ear trumpet closer.

"Beautiful," shouted the children again.

Oswald straightened up and took the trumpet from his ear and peered into it.

"Won't be a moment," he said to the children, "technical trouble."

He pushed one of his long claws into the ear trumpet and scrabbled about. Then he shook the trumpet and a large quantity of icing sugar fell out.

"There," he said, pleased. "It gets a little bit choked up occasionally."

He put it back in his ear, and Parrot flew up and perched on it. "Can you hear me now?" he asked Oswald.

"Perfectly," said Oswald, surprised. "But then I could hear you before. All that nonsense about a goat."

"Well, listen carefully," said Parrot. "It's essential that we get to Werewolf Island as quickly as possible."

"Werewolf Island?" said Oswald. "What on earth do you want to go there for? Nasty place, nasty people. I went there sunbathing not long ago and the Werewolves threw stones at me. Nasty, vulgar creatures."

"Well, the reason we want to go there is a long story

which we haven't got time to tell you now," said Parrot. "But we must get there before moonrise; now can you give us a tow?"

"Simplest thing in the world," said Oswald. "You got a rope in the crumpet, I take it? Well, slip it round my neck and away we go."

So they tied the painter round Oswald's neck and set off. At first, in his enthusiasm to help, Oswald went far too fast and the dinghy bounced up and down so much they were all nearly thrown out. Needless to say, Oswald had put his ear trumpet away, so he couldn't hear them shouting to slow down, and in the end Parrot had to fly up to his nose and peck him before he became aware of what he was doing. At last, he got the speed right and they zoomed across the waves at a tremendous rate.

"Tell me," asked Simon, "why does Oswald wear that chef's hat?"

"He *is* a chef," said Parrot. "Studied in Paris and China. Excellent cook, Oswald; but his father wouldn't let him continue with it: said cooking wasn't for Sea Serpents. So he made poor Oswald give it up and go into the family business."

"What family business?" asked Penelope.

"It's a firm Oswald's great-great-grandfather started, called 'Excitement Unlimited'. If there are places not very popular with tourists, well they just send one of their family there for a bit. He lets himself be seen and photographed a couple of times and, before you know it, the place is crammed with people wanting to see the Sea Serpent. But Oswald's a very shy creature and he doesn't like the publicity involved, and he's a kindly soul, so he doesn't like leaving footprints in people's back gardens or breathing on picnic parties, suddenly, from behind rocks. No, what he wanted really to do was to open a restaurant, but his father said 'whoever had heard of a Sea Serpent running a restaurant?' so

Oswald had to join the firm and he does his cooking as a hobby."

"Poor Oswald," said Penelope.

"Yes, it's a shame," said Peter. "It must be horrid to have to go round, showing off when you're modest."

"Yes, particularly if he's a good cook," said Simon.

"One of the very best," said Parrot, "and won't use Moon-carrots – oh no, insists on fresh ingredients. Very particular is Oswald."

Now the sky was starting to go a deep golden green, and the children could see the beginnings of the four sunsets. On the horizon a mere smudge at first and then getting clearer and clearer loomed Werewolf Island.

"I don't think we'll do it before sunset," said Parrot looking at his watch, and then at the sun which was sinking towards the horizon. "We'll have to go ashore in the dark, but we must be off there by moonrise, whatever happens. It was so silly of me not to think of it, but we *could* have got H.H. to keep the sun shining for two days. But you always think of these things too late."

As they got closer to the Island, it began to look more and more unfriendly with craggy rocks and straggling bushes. It looked dark and evil, and Penelope shivered as she remembered what lived on it.

"We'll land on the south end, I've told Oswald," Parrot explained, "because the Mandrake Forest is in the north-east and the Werewolves' lairs in the north-west. If we can get through the Mandrakes without waking them or the Wolves smelling us, we should have the rue and be out again in next to no time."

"What about the Will-o-the-Wisps?" asked Peter.

"Oh, they're all right, just mischievous. You can't trust them," said Parrot.

Oswald had slowed down as they neared the Island, and now headed for a little cove where they beached the dinghy on the sand, which was red and black and glowed uncannily in the light of the sunset.

"Now, remember," Parrot said to Penelope. "You stay here with Ethelred and Oswald, and at the first sign of any trouble put out to sea."

"And what about you?" protested Penelope.

"Never mind about us," said Parrot confidently. "We'll be all right."

"Good-bye Penelope," whispered Peter. "Remember, any danger and you scoot off."

"Yes," said Simon, "don't take any risks."

"Good-bye," said Penelope. "You take care, too."

Carrying the sacks and the sickles, Peter and Simon and Parrot made their way down through the bushes, as quietly as they could.

Penelope sat down on the beach with Ethelred beside her and Oswald lying in the shallows.

"Don't you worry, miss," said Ethelred, comfortingly. "Why, they'll be through that 'orrid Mandrake wood and into the rue field before you can say 'fried frogs' spawn'."

Oswald had been listening to this with great attention through his ear trumpet. "Tell me," he said, "what do they want the rue for?"

"To give it to them Weasels, of course," said Ethelred.

"To give it to the Weasels? Yes, of course, how stupid of me not to have thought of that," said Oswald. "Why?"

"Cor blimey, don't you know anything?" asked Ethelred. "Don't you know about the Cockatrices and all that?"

"No, I'm sorry I don't," said Oswald, apologetically. "I've been on a mission, you see, and I've only just got back."

So, as much to while away the time as anything, Penelope and Ethelred told him about the Cockatrices and their adventures.

"Audacious brutes," said Oswald when they had finished. "To think of them doing that to H.H., the kindest of men. A man who gave me my very *best* recipe for raspberry flan. How lucky he had you to help him."

"So you see," said Penelope, "if we can just get the rue, it might solve everything."

"Yes, indeed, I see how important it is," said Oswald. "It is, as it were, like the final pinch of pepper, the thimble of salt, the fragment of onion, or the merest, tiny, tichy, teensy-weensy tridgle of herbs that makes all the difference between success or failure in a recipe."

"*Exactly*," said Penelope. "How well you put it."

"I don't understand a word he's on about," Ethelred confessed.

"I wonder," said Oswald, "whether I ought to swim round to the north-east of the Island, so that I would be, as it were, on hand in case of an emergency?"

"Oh, *would* you?" said Penelope, eagerly. "That would be comforting."

"Well, in that case, I'll be off," said Oswald, and he swam out into the bay, submerged and disappeared as swiftly and as silently as a minnow.

Penelope and Ethelred sat silent on the sand by the dinghy for what seemed like hours.

"It's a pity we 'ave to be quiet, miss," whispered Ethelred at length, "else I would have sung to you. Us Toads are famous for our voices, you know, and I know some lovely songs, 'onest I do."

"That's very kind of you," said Penelope. "I would have appreciated it very much."

"If I'd brought me conjuror's outfit, I could have shown you some tricks," he went on, " 'cause I was a conjuror before I became a spy, see. I can produce a newt out o' me top 'at in a way that would baffle anyone."

"I'm sure you can," said Penelope.

They sat in silence again while Penelope imagined all

the awful things that might be happening to Peter, Simon and Parrot.

"Tell you wot, miss," said Ethelred at last. "You see that there little 'ill at the end of the bay? Well, if I was to climb that I could see a good bit of the Island, and I dare say, more than likely, that I'd see them coming back, laden down with the rue. Shall I take an 'op up there, miss?"

"All right," said Penelope. "I can see no harm in it, but I'd better stay and guard the boat."

"Right you are, miss, back in a jiffy," whispered Ethelred and hopped off.

Without Ethelred, the night seemed twice as dark and lonely, and Penelope was just beginning to wish she had not allowed him to go when two things happened that made her wish even more that Ethelred was with her. First, over the very rim of the Singing Sea the first, tiny edge of the moon appeared, like a curved shred of silver. Swiftly it rose and in a moment or two it was clear of the Sea and flooding everything with a silvery light. The moment the moon had risen and was floating clear of the sky, Penelope heard echoing and re-echoing a series of long-drawn-out blood-curdling howls. Gradually, they died away and silence fell again. A silence that seemed even more horrid, because she knew now that the Were-wolves had woken up and were on the prowl. She was just wondering whether to go in search of Ethelred when she heard another noise. At first, it seemed like a very faint sigh, soft and far away; then, as it grew closer, she could distinguish words.

"Help me," said the voice, so faint and as soft as thistle-down. "Please help me, please."

Penelope got to her feet and went quickly up the beach to where the bushes began, for it was here that the voice seemed to come from. At first, she could see nothing in the gloom and then suddenly she saw a light, a strange, rainbow-coloured light that seemed to be rolling or dragging itself through the bushes towards the beach.

"Help me, please, help me," came the tiny, pathetic voice.

And it seemed to Penelope that it came from the strange light that came towards her along the ground. Without a thought of the danger, Penelope ran straight through the bushes towards the light. When she got close to it, she saw that it was about the size of a tennis ball and appeared to be composed entirely of multi-coloured candle flames and yet, when she looked closely, she saw that it was a small, round, fat bird with a beak like a duck whose plumage, instead of being feathers, appeared to be highly coloured flames. The flames flickered to and fro so much that it was difficult to see exactly what the creature looked like, but one thing was obvious and that was that it was very sick. Penelope ran forward and bent down to pick it up in her hands, when the creature rolled on to its back and pushed her hands away with two frail claws like a robin's.

"Don't touch me," it gasped faintly. "Wait while I change."

Penelope drew back her hand and watched. To her astonishment, the creature suddenly turned from being every colour under the sun to being a pale whitish-yellow.

"Now I'm cold," it said in a faint voice. "Now you may pick me up."

Penelope bent forward and gathered up the strange creature in her hand. It was as light as thistledown and it throbbed gently as if she were holding a bird. She turned and made her way back to the beach with it. When she reached the dinghy she sat down on the sand and put the strange creature into her lap. It settled back with a sigh of relief.

"You must be Penelope," it said, "hic."

"Yes," said Penelope, "that's right. But how did you know? And who are you?"

"I'm a Firedrake," panted the little creature. "At least, hic, I'm not quite, really I'm a Fire Duckling. I was only hatched a week ago – hic. My name's Fenella."

"But what happened to you?" asked Penelope.

"I must tell you quickly," gasped Fenella. "There's no time – hic – to lose. I was out this evening practising my flying – hic – just as the sun went down and I happened to land in a bush. I'm not very good yet, you see – hic – and all my lights went out because I was stunned. When I came to – hic – there was a group of Will-o-the-Wisps near the bush I was in – hic – and they were plotting. You know what – hic – plotters the Will-o-the-Wisps are. But this was really a *nasty* plot. They said that two humans and Mr Parrot – hic – were making their way across the Island and they'd left a Toad and a Penelope (I suppose that's you?) in charge of the boat. They said – hic – they were going to tell the Werewolves where Mr Parrot and the others were – hic – and then when they were all together they were going to wake the Mandrakes – hic."

"Did they indeed," said Penelope, thoroughly enraged. "Nasty, spiteful, plotting things. Then what happened?"

"Well, then I got hiccups," said Fenella apologetically, "and they all rushed at me – hic – and started banging me about, and I fell out of the bush and broke my wing – hic. Then they got frightened and ran away. But I thought I ought to come – hic – here to warn you. I hope I did right?"

"Absolutely right," said Penelope, and she was so angry at what the Will-o-the-Wisps had done to Fenella that her voice shook. "Now, I'll tell you what *I'm* going to do. I'm going to put you safely in the boat and you're to wait for a Toad to come – his name is Ethelred. When he comes, tell him what you've told me and tell him I've gone to warn Mr Parrot. Can you remember that?"

"Oh yes," said Fenella. "I've a very good – hic – memory. It's just my flying that's bad – hic."

"And when I come back, I'll mend your wing," said Penelope.

"Do take care," said Fenella. "Those Will-o-the-Wisps – hic – aren't to be trusted, truly."

"I'll take care," said Penelope, putting Fenella carefully into the boat. "Now, are you comfortable?"

"Yes, thank you – hic – very much," said Fenella.

"Well, just stay there and wait for Ethelred," said Penelope.

And taking the torch, she made her way rapidly up the beach and into the bushes. There was a rough track that was obviously the way Parrot and the boys had gone. She pushed on through the bushes and presently they gave way to a rather dry, scratchy sort of grassland and ahead of her loomed a wood. This must be the Mandrake Forest, she thought, and remembered that the important thing was not to wake them. When she had tiptoed to the edge of the forest, she stopped and turned on her torch for a moment, for she wanted to see what the Mandrakes were like. What she saw in her torch beam made her want to giggle. They were all shaped like great, green Easter eggs with large eyes that were tightly shut, large ears, snub noses and pouting sulky mouths on their trunks. From each side of their trunks stuck two short, stubby branches ending in a bunch of twigs and leaves which were presumably the Mandrake's equivalent to arms and hands. On their heads, like a tangled wig, were more short branches and a lot of leaves. As they slept they all snored gently so that the whole forest vibrated. Penelope switched off the torch and tiptoed through the Mandrakes and into the wood. She had to move with great caution, using only the pale light of the moon to see by, for she did not want to walk into a Mandrake by mistake or tread on a twig that would wake them up. So step by step she made her way slowly and carefully through the snoring Mandrakes.

Presently, she came to a clearing in the forest that was flooded with moonlight, and from it led six paths in different directions. Then she noticed in the gloom, among the Mandrakes, around the clearing several greeny-blue lights that pulsed but remained quite stationary, as if they were watching her. It was the Will-o-the-Wisps, and soon she could hear their sniggering, soft voices talking to each other.

"That's her, that's her," sniggered one.

"Yes yes, yes yes," chorused the others.

"She can't find her way-a-y . . ." giggled the first one.

"No, she can't, she can't, she's lost," they chorused.

"Soon she'll be eaten."

"Yes yes, yes yes."

"Eaten, eaten, eaten."

"Yes yes, yes yes."

Penelope was so angry that she longed to shout at the Will-o-the-Wisps and tell them what she thought of them, but she didn't dare for fear of waking the Mandrakes. Then, as suddenly as they had appeared, the Will-o-the-Wisps slipped off through the trees and were gone. Penelope stood in the centre of the clearing and wondered which one of the six paths to choose, wishing she had a compass with her. She closed her eyes and tried to remember the map of the Island and in which direction the rue field lay. When she opened her eyes, at the entrance to each path stood a Werewolf.

They looked like very large, shaggy Alsatian dogs, walking on their hind legs and using their front paws as cleverly as a monkey. Their eyes glinted green in the moonlight and they were all panting, their red tongues flapping in and out, their white teeth gleaming. Before Penelope could do anything, the Werewolves converged on her swiftly and silently. A bag was thrown over her head and she felt herself lifted in hard, furry paws, and carried off, the only sound being the hoarse panting of her captors, as they jogged along.

Presently, they arrived at their destination. Penelope was put down and tied to what felt like a tree trunk. Then the bag was removed from her head and she saw she was in a large, gloomy cave lit by a big, flickering fire. She had been bound to a tree trunk that had been planted upright in the cave's earthen floor, and on either side of her were two other tree trunks and to them were tied Peter and Simon.

"Penelope!" exclaimed Peter. "What are you doing here?"

"Why aren't you with Oswald?" cried Simon.

Hastily, since the Werewolves had left the cave, Penelope related her story of the Firedrake and her subsequent capture.

'Well," said Peter, "we got through the Mandrake Forest all right and we found the rue – it grows just on the sea shore near here."

"We put it into the sacks," said Simon, "and then Oswald appeared and said you'd sent him. So we told him to go back and get the dinghy and you and Ethelred."

"Parrot went with him," said Peter, "and we were waiting for you to come back, when suddenly a whole host of those awful Wisps appeared, shouting: 'Here they are, here they are,' and the Werewolves jumped on us before we could do anything. That was half an hour ago."

"What are they going to do with us?" asked Penelope.

"Turn us into Werewolves," answered Peter gloomily, "to increase their numbers."

"Don't be silly, how could they?" said Penelope aghast.

"Yes, they can," said Simon. "If they bite us, we'll turn into Werewolves. The guard told us. They're having a special ceremony when the moon sets, when they'll bite us and that'll be that."

Penelope was silent, thinking of the fate awaiting them.

"Well, we can't get free, we've tried," said Peter. "They certainly know how to tie you up."

"I've got a knife in my pocket, but I can't reach it," said Simon.

Just at that moment a Werewolf came into the cave Seen in the flickering firelight they were even more fierce looking and unattractive than they had been by moonlight, Penelope decided.

"No talking," said the Werewolf in a harsh, growly voice. "I've told you before."

"Oh, go and boil your head," said Peter pugnaciously

"Yes," said Simon, "we've got every right to talk, why shouldn't we?"

"It's the law," said the Werewolf, lying down by the fire.

"How can it be the law when you haven't had any prisoners before?" asked Penelope, indignantly. "Don't be so stupid."

The Werewolf put his ears back and snarled at her. "We're not stupid," he said. "We captured you *all* and that was not stupid, so be quiet."

There was silence for a time, only broken by the crackling of the fire. Then, suddenly, the Werewolf, who'd been lying dozing with his head on his paws, pricked up his ears. Then he sat up, staring at the mouth of the cave. Looking, the children could see something very strange creeping into the cave. It looked like a long, white caterpillar. The children and the Werewolf watched it, as it crawled steadily closer and closer to the fire. The Werewolf got up on all fours, the fur on his back standing up and he growled at the strange, white caterpillar-like thing.

"Halt, who goes there?" he snarled.

"Arr," said the caterpillar, "Arr, arr, friend."

"Who are you?" said the Werewolf, now somewhat alarmed.

"I'm a Weretoad," said a well-known voice. "I'm a Weretoad, and I've been sent 'ere with a very important present for the Chief of the Werewolves."

As this strange apparition got close to the fire, the delighted children could see that it was indeed Ethelred with a large roll of cotton wool stuck to his back.

"What's a Weretoad?" asked the Werewolf, puzzled.

"You mean to say you've never *'eard* of a Weretoad?" asked Ethelred with scorn. "I don't think much of *your* education, then."

"I'm very well educated," said the Werewolf, indignantly.

"Well educated? You? You, wot's never 'eard of a Weretoad?" said Ethelred. "Lummy, if I was you, I'd be ashamed to admit I didn't know wot a Weretoad was."

"Well, what is it?" asked the Werewolf, angrily.

"It's just like a Werewolf, only different," said Ethelred. "More dangerous like, more evil and cunning."

"You couldn't be more dangerous or evil or cunning than *us*," said the Werewolf, indignantly. "I don't believe you."

"Are you accusing me of telling lies?" inquired Ethelred. "I do 'ope not for your sake. We Weretoads can be real nasty if we're put upon."

"I'm not saying you're lying," said the Werewolf, hastily. "I just said I didn't believe you."

"Well, that's better then," said Ethelred. "Now where's your Chief, eh? I've got this present for 'im."

"What is the present?" asked the Werewolf, suspiciously.

"Look, it's for 'im not for you," said Ethelred. "It's a special magic potion for making Were-things twice as

. . . er . . . um . . . er, twice as 'Were' as wot they are, see?"

"Twice as 'Were'?" asked the Werewolf. "You mean more cunning, more dangerous, more evil?"

"Yes, that's it," said Ethelred, producing a small bottle from under his cotton-wool disguise. "You just rub this 'ere lotion on your tail, and before you can say 'filleted frog's legs', you've become one of the 'Were-iest' of all Werewolves."

"You mean that if . . . just supposing, of course . . . if I had this potion I could be promoted – say – from sentry to leader of the pack?" asked the Werewolf, licking his lips.

"Of course," said Ethelred. "No doubt about it. Shouldn't be surprised but wot your Chief doesn't proclaim himself king after rubbing that lot on his tail."

"There . . . er . . . seems to be a great *deal* in that bottle," said the Werewolf, thoughtfully.

"Yes," said Ethelred, "plenty 'ere."

"I wondered if . . . perhaps . . . you might allow me to just put the tiniest bit on my tail?" said the Werewolf. "I mean just the merest drop – so little, the Chief wouldn't notice."

"Well, I don't know about *that* now," said Ethelred, doubtfully. "After all, it's 'is present, and I 'aven't got no right, really."

"Oh go on," said the Werewolf, pleadingly. "Just a drop – he'll never know, and I'll be ever so grateful."

"Well," said Ethelred, reluctantly. "Arr . . . you're only to 'ave a drop, mind, you promise?"

"Yes, oh yes, I promise," said the Werewolf, "only a drop."

"All right then," said Ethelred.

He held out the bottle to the Werewolf who snatched it from him, pulled out the cork and immediately poured the entire contents of the bottle over his tail. The children could smell the strong, pungent odour of surgical spirit which they knew was kept in the Red-Cross box for cleaning up cuts and bruises.

"Ah *ha*," smiled the Werewolf, triumphantly. "I've fooled you, I've put it *all* on. Now, I'll be King of the Werewolves, now I'll be more *evil*, more *dangerous*, more *horrible* than anyone else. Now I shall start by eating you, you miserable Weretoad, you."

"Well, we'll see about that," said Ethelred, and picked up a flaming branch from the fire and threw it on to the Werewolf's tail. Immediately, the surgical spirits caught fire and the Werewolf's whole tail burst into flame.

"Arr . . ." screamed the Werewolf, "my tail! my tail!"

"Burning a treat it is," said Ethelred.

"Ow ow ow! . . ." yelled the Werewolf, running round and round the fire. "My tail! my tail!"

"I should go and stick it in the sea, if I were you," advised Ethelred. "Cool it orf like."

Still screaming with pain, the Werewolf took his advice and ran out of the cave and disappeared in the direction of the sea, his tail streaming like a bonfire behind him.

"That's got 'im all 'ot and bothered," said Ethelred in triumph, tearing off his cotton-wool disguise. "Now a bit of the old rescue."

"Ethelred, you're wonderful," said Penelope.

"Terrific," said Peter.

"Marvellous," said Simon.

"Well, now," said Ethelred blushing, "it was nuffink really. Just wot we Master Spies are trained to do. 'Ere, I don't think I can untie them knots, though."

"There's a penknife in my pocket," said Simon.

"How on earth did you find us?" asked Penelope.

Ethelred had opened the knife and was busily cutting them free. "Well," he said, "when I got back to the boat and found you'd gone, I nearly 'ad a fit, and when that stupid, hiccupping bird told me wot she told you and wot you were going to do, well I nearly 'ad *two* fits, and that's a fact."

He cut Penelope free and she was rubbing her wrists where the ropes had chafed her. Now he turned his attention to Peter.

"Well, miss," he went on, "I hopped after you as quick as ever I could, but you don't 'alf walk fast. Anyway, I just caught up with you in the Mandrake Forest there, where all them paths were. I was just about to give you a shout when, cor lummy, all them 'orrors jumps on you."

He cut Peter free and turned to Simon.

"Well, I'll tell you straight," Ethelred confessed, "I couldn't 'ave fought them all. I'd 'ave tried them one at a time like, but these things don't fight like that. So I just followed them 'ere, and then when the others went off to arrange 'The Great Biting' as they called it, they left that silly one in 'ere on 'is own, I said Ethelred me lad, I said, this is where your mastery over the hart of disguise is going to pay orf. But then I remembered I 'adn't got me disguises – all there was in the Red-Cross box was that there cotton-wool and that smelly stuff, so I 'ad to do the best I could."

"You're wonderfully brave," said Penelope.

"Brilliantly intelligent," said Peter.

"Incredibly resourceful," said Simon.

" 'Ang on a bit," said Ethelred, "you'll 'ave me blushing again."

"No one else in the world could have done as well," said Penelope with conviction.

"Well, come on," said Peter. "We'd better get out of here before the wretched animals come back."

So, with great caution, they made their way out of the cave, through the Mandrake Forest, and then through the field of rue, down to the sea. In the distance they could hear the howling of the Werewolves, which made

161

Penelope shiver. When they reached the beach, they walked along it, while Peter and Simon tried to find the landmark where they were supposed to meet Parrot. Suddenly Penelope, glancing over her shoulder, gave a gasp of horror. "Look," she said. "The Werewolves."

At the far end of the beach, running on all fours, came the Werewolf pack, their eyes glinting, their tongues flapping like flags, their teeth gleaming white as mushrooms in the moonlight. They had their noses to the ground and were following the children's tracks.

"Let's get round the promontory into the next bay," said Peter, "and Simon and I will try to hold them off with rocks, while you and Ethelred find the boat."

They ran towards the promontory and started to scramble over the rocks. Then Peter, who was leading, suddenly stopped. "Hush," he whispered. "There's something the other side of these rocks. Perhaps the Werewolves have another pack and have sent it round to cut us off?"

They all stopped, their hearts beating, and listened. For a moment there was silence, and then a voice said: "For a really delicious shepherd's pie I always use a pinch of rosemary and thyme, as well as sage and onions, and the merest dash of the best Madeira."

"Do you – hic – really," said another voice.

"It's Oswald!" cried Penelope, "Oswald and Fenella."

They scrambled over the rocks and there below them was the dinghy with Parrot and Fenella on board, and Oswald lying in the shallows.

Behind them, they could hear the panting and snarling of the Werewolves and the clattering of the falling rocks, as the pack pursued them. Quickly the children and Ethelred jumped down from the rock on to the beach in the next bay and ran towards the dinghy.

"Parrot, Parrot help!" shouted Penelope. "The Werewolves are after us."

"Werewolves," said Oswald. "Werewolves? We'll soon see about that."

He surged down the bay and slid out on to the beach, putting his great kingfisher-blue body between the children and the Werewolves. Then he sucked up a great mouthful of seawater and spat it at the Werewolf pack, like a fire hose. This hard jet of water caught the leading Werewolves and bowled them over and over, yelping and snarling.

"Nasty, ill-mannered, stone-throwing beasts," said Oswald and he filled his mouth again and spat another jet of water at the Werewolves, who were now in full retreat. Meanwhile Parrot had flown on to Penelope's shoulder, and kissed her ear.

"Dearest, dearest Penelope," he said, "how glad I am that you are safe. Quick into the boat all of you."

They scrambled into the dinghy and pushed off, and when they were far enough from shore, they called to Oswald, who was thoroughly enjoying himself, chasing the Werewolves up and down the beach, spitting water at them. At length he left the pack, drenched, bruised and angry, and swam out to join the dinghy.

"That will teach them," he said with satisfaction. "That'll teach them not to throw stones at strangers."

"Well," chortled Parrot as the boys fixed the rope round Oswald's neck, "we've done it, by Jove. Everybody safe, and four sacks of rue. How's that for a triumphant, piece of work?"

"We can stop on the way to get some lavender," said Peter. "Then – Cockatrices – watch out."

"Yes," said Simon, "we'll show them."

"Is Oswald going to pull us all the way back?" asked Penelope.

"Yes," said Oswald. "You're just fortunate that I have nothing in the oven at the moment, so a day either way won't matter."

"Good," said Penelope, "because I've got some recipes to give you."

"Oh you are a kind and generous maiden," said Oswald.

"Well, off we go," said Parrot.

And so Oswald surged ahead and swam towards the rising sun, pulling the dinghy behind him, taking the children on the last stage of their strange adventure.

eight

THE BATTLE FOR COCKATRICE CASTLE

As soon as the party made their way back to the Crystal Caves with the precious lavender and rue, a period of intense activity took place. To begin with, Ethelred, Peter and Simon all had brilliant ideas. Ethelred's idea was that they should enlist the aid of Oswald and the Mermaids, to pull out the great plug at the bottom of the moat of Cockatrice Castle. Once the water level had dropped, as Ethelred pointed out, it would expose any number of large drains which led into the dungeon area where the Great Books were kept. What everyone was afraid of was that when they were attacked the Cockatrices might burn up the Great Books out of spite, and without them, H.H. was powerless. So, Ethelred's idea was that a picked group of creatures should make their way up the drains, overpower the sentries and guard the Great Books from harm until the Castle was taken. Everyone agreed that this was a splendid plan, and so Oswald had been despatched to see Miss Williamson-Smythe-Smythe-Browne, to explain the whole thing and enlist the aid of the mermaids.

Simon's and Peter's idea had come to them when watching Fenella. With the aid of some sealing wax and string and a candle flame, the three children had managed to mend the Fire Duckling's wing which, in a remarkably short space of time, had healed. Simon and Peter were having a conference on the best way of besieging Cockatrice Castle, and watching Fenella as she jumped off the back of a chair and practised flying round the room.

"What we really want is an aeroplane, so that we can drop people inside the Castle itself," said Peter.

"What about balloons?" suggested Simon.

"Balloons?" asked Peter. "Where would we get them?"

"Make them – Mooncalf jelly."

"But how would they float?" asked Peter.

"Well," said Simon, "you know that hot air rises. So why don't we fill the balloons with hot air?"

"But how?" asked Peter, puzzled.

"Firedrakes," said Simon. "You know how *hot* Fenella is. Well, if we could get, say, twenty Firedrakes inside a balloon it would float, and what's more I believe they could steer it by flapping their wings and all flying in the right direction."

The boys were very excited with this idea, and so was Fenella at the thought of helping. So they made a small experimental balloon and Fenella got into it. To Simon's delight it worked perfectly and Fenella could make the balloon fly round and round the room as she wanted. She was so overcome at her achievement that she got an attack of hiccups.

"I did it – hic – didn't I Simon – hic?" she said delightedly. "Did you – hic – see me turn at that – hic – corner, Peter?"

"You were wonderful," Peter assured her.

"Now the thing is, how many Firedrakes are there?" asked Simon.

"Oh, hundreds – hic – " said Fenella. "At *least* – hic – two hundred, if not more."

"Could you get them to join us?" asked Simon.

"I'm sure I could – hic – " said Fenella. "After I tell them how kind – hic – you've been to me, and how important it all is – hic – hic."

"Well, could you go and ask them to join us here at the Crystal Caves?" asked Simon. "Tell them this is going to be our headquarters for the big attack."

So, Fenella, overjoyed at having a task of such immense importance to undertake, flew off, hiccupping, to enlist the aid of the Firedrakes.

In the meantime, Parrot and the children had paid another visit to Weaseldom where Wensleydale greeted them warmly. He was having tea on the croquet lawn with Winifred.

"Did you get it, did you get it?" he shrilled, jumping up and down in excitement. "My, I'm so excited. How I wish my lumbago had not prevented me from coming with you."

"We got plenty of rue," said Parrot, "but H.H. is keeping it under lock and key. We don't want you Weasels getting out of hand like the Cockatrices. So H.H. just made up one big bottle of it."

"Silly *billy*," said Wensleydale, "as if *we* would get out of hand, you know what quiet, peace-loving creatures we Weasels are."

"Well, we're not taking any chances," said Parrot. "Here's the rue juice, then. Who's going to try it, you?"

"Normally, I would be *delighted*," said Wensleydale, "but – Arr, Ouch, Ooo, I still have a *touch* of my lumbago, Ooooo. I don't think it would be safe. No, I think it would be better to try it on the under-gardener. He's a nice lad but a very bad gardener, so if the stuff did turn out to be – er . . . er . . . well, *you* know, dangerous in any way, it wouldn't be such a loss."

"It's not dangerous, you ninny," said Parrot. "Do you think H.H. hasn't tested it?"

"All the same," said Wensleydale, nervously, "it had better be the under-gardener. He's *so* looking forward to it and I wouldn't like to disappoint him."

So the under-gardener, whose name was Wilberforce,

was sent for. They stood him in the middle of the croquet lawn for the experiment.

"Now, Wilberforce," said Parrot, "you understand this stuff is quite harmless, but after you've drunk it you're to tell me if you feel any different, you understand?"

"Yes sir," said Wilberforce, who wore a bowler hat, large horn-rimmed spectacles, had stick-out teeth and a runny nose. "You're going to drink that stuff, and I'm going to tell you if it makes me feel any better. Thank you, sir."

"You see what I mean," said Wensleydale in despair. "Only the other day he pulled up *all* my daffodil bulbs and took them round to the kitchen, because he thought they were potatoes."

"You haven't got it quite right," said Parrot. "*You*, Wilberforce, are going to drink this and then *you*, Wilberforce, will tell me if you feel better. Do you understand?"

"Oh yes, sir," said Wilberforce.

He took the bottle and gulped down a swig of it.

"It's a very curious name – Wilberforce," whispered Peter to Simon, as they waited for something to happen.

"Very odd," Simon agreed.

Wilberforce stood there, blinking through his spectacles, and they all watched him. For over five minutes he appeared to be exactly the same, and their hearts sank; had they been to so much trouble and so much danger for nothing?

"How do you feel?" asked Parrot.

Wilberforce blinked at him.

"I said, how do you feel?" asked Parrot loudly.

"I heard you the first time; there's no need to *shout*," said Wilberforce. "And what's it got to do with *you* how I feel, eh? Mind your own business, you interfering bird, or I'll knock your beak off."

"Good gracious," said Peter in astonishment.

"And as for *you* two," Wilberforce went on, striding

across the lawn and shouting up at them. "What right have *you* got to insult my name? Put your faces down here, and I'll knock them through the back of your heads."

"Good heavens, this is most miraculous," said Wensleydale. "I've never seen anything like it!"

Wilberforce wheeled round and, before anybody knew what he was doing, he had seized Wensleydale by his lace cravat and was shaking him to and fro.

"As for you," shouted Wilberforce, "I'm sick and tired of you, you and your pernickety ways, that I am, and it's about time someone taught you a lesson, that it is."

So saying, Wilberforce hit Wensleydale, Duke of Weaseldom, so hard in the eye that it knocked him back, so that he hit the tea-trolley and upset it. The children gazed in astonishment at Wensleydale lying there covered in buttered toast and meringues, while Wilberforce danced around him.

"Get up and fight, you coward," shouted Wilberforce, "you lily-livered white ermine you, get up, and I'll cut you to pieces, so I will. I'll cut both your ears off, and knock all your teeth out."

It took the other six gardeners all their time to subdue Wilberforce and to lock him in the gardeners' shed.

"I think," said Parrot, as they watched a moaning Wensleydale being carried into the house. "I think that experiment is what you might call an unqualified, universal and ubiquitous success, don't you?"

The children agreed whole-heartedly.

When Wensleydale recovered a bit (although his eye was very swollen), he promised that the whole of Weaseldom would now join the fight of the Cockatrices, so the children and Parrot went jubilantly back to the Crystal Caves.

Now the Crystal Caves were all bustle, chatter and work.

The Griffons had rounded up a herd of the Moon-calves and established them in one of the side tunnels, where they produced sheet after sheet of Moon-calf jelly which Penelope, Dulcibelle and H.H. thought into balloons and other things that they would need. Out in a secluded Moon-carrot meadow Peter, now in his element, was training his battalion of Unicorn cavalry, teaching them to trot, canter, wheel all together as one unit. The Unicorns seemed very quick at learning, and before long Peter was really proud of their precision and skill.

For several days Ethelred had been missing for long periods, and, although they had noticed, they had been too busy to give it much thought. Then he appeared one day just as Penelope had thought vast quantities of Moon-calf jelly into seven hundred fire-proof suits for the Weasels and was feeling rather exhausted. To her astonishment, Ethelred was wearing a tricorne hat and a very smart uniform with gold epaulettes and all sorts of gold braid round the sleeves. The coat was a very deep bottle green and the trousers were white. He was wearing a large sword with a silver scabbard.

"Why Ethelred, you look magnificent," said Penelope.

" 'Opes you likes it," said Ethelred. "It's me Commander-in-chief's uniform."

"Really?" said Penelope. "What are you Commander-in-chief of?"

"Come with me and I'll show you," said Ethelred.

And he led her into one of the side tunnels. There to Penelope's surprise and delight, some fifty Toads stood to attention, each wearing a lovely scarlet uniform with brass buttons, pill-box hats with big, black feathers in them, and carrying long, sharply pointed pikes and bows and arrows. When they saw Penelope, they all stood smartly to attention.

"But where did they come from?" she said, bewildered.

"Cockatrice Castle," said Ethelred. "I didn't want to be the only Toad 'elping you all, so I slipped down there, disguised as a Greek ship owner with forty-two galleons to 'ire, and made all me relatives join."

"Why, that's splendid," said Penelope, warmly. "I know that H.H. will be simply delighted."

Ethelred took off his tricorne hat and cleared his throat. "With your permission, miss, I'd like to christen this bunch – er . . . brigade – Miss Penelope's Terrifying Toad Brigade."

"Of course, you may, that's most flattering," said Penelope.

"Thank you, miss," said Ethelred gratified. "I'm just taking them out for a little archery practice, so if you'd be so kind as to take the salute, like?"

"Of course," said Penelope.

"Brigade, shun!" shouted Ethelred. All the Toads in their red uniforms stood to attention.

"Right wheel," shouted Ethelred, "quick march."

The Brigade obeyed him.

As they marched past Penelope, Ethelred shouted: "Eyes Right," and Penelope stood smartly to attention, saluting.

"Thank you, miss," said Ethelred when the Brigade had marched away.

"I'm going to give them some target practice now. Some of 'em ain't alf bad shots. One of them yesterday nearly put a harrow through me 'at."

Peter and Simon spent a lot of time in H.H.'s extensive library reading up on the best method of attacking castles, and in one book they came across an illustration of a machine which they thought might well be useful. It was a form of giant catapult with a long arm, rather like a soup spoon. You pulled the arm back, put your ammunition in the bowl of the spoon and then released it. So, between them, the boys thought up (out of Moon-calf jelly) one of these catapults, as an experiment, and it seemed to work. The problem was what to fire out of them, and it was the Griffons who solved this. They suggested they make golden cannon balls. Not only did these prove to be a great success, but the Griffons turned out to be very good shots.

Meanwhile, Fenella had returned from Werewolf Island, bringing with her all her friends and relatives. Penelope and the boys watched them fly in one evening after dark, and they agreed it was one of the most beautiful sights they had seen in Mythologia, as the Firedrakes came flying over the moonlit sea in a long, wavering, multi-coloured ribbon that looked as though a very vivid rainbow had come to life. As soon as they were installed in the Crystal Caves, Simon began experiments with his balloons. He found that it required forty Firedrakes for a balloon to have enough power to lift a basket containing thirty fully-armed Weasels. So he could have a fleet of fifteen balloons. The balloons were a great success and the Firedrakes took tremendous pride in the way they could manoeuvre them through the sky.

So everything was made ready: the corridors were full of drilling Toads and Weasels, the Griffons and Tabitha worked hard manufacturing great piles of golden cannon balls, and Penelope spent hours attaching the baskets to the balloons with specially thick silk which Dulcibelle had spun for the purpose. On the day before the attack Simon wanted to show everybody, with the aid of a large model he had made of Cockatrice Castle, exactly what they would have to do. The problem was to find a place to assemble them all.

"Oh, that's easy," said H.H. when Simon put the problem to him. "Use the banqueting hall."

"I didn't know you had one," said Simon.

"Oh yes," said H.H. "Come and I'll show you."

He led Simon along several corridors and threw open

huge, double doors, and there was an immense room with a beautifully polished crystal floor, lit by hundreds of wonderful mushroom chandeliers.

"Why, it's *perfect*," said Simon in delight. "We can even fit Oswald in here."

"It will be nice to have it used," said H.H. "I built it originally so that we could have balls and banquets indoors, should it rain, quite forgetting, of course, that I'm in charge of the weather here, so if I don't want it to rain, it doesn't. So it's never been used, which is a pity."

"Well, we'll make good use of it now," said Simon.

The day before the big attack everybody assembled in the great banqueting hall. There were rows and rows of excited Weasels and Toads, and a great clattering, head-nodding group of Unicorns, a solid wedge of Griffons, their leather aprons all glittering with specks and splashes of melted gold from the cannon balls. There was a great, quivering, squeaking mass of Firedrakes, like a huge, moving flower-bed. There was Miss Williamson-Smythe-Smythe-Browne and her young ladies (who had been transported there on Oswald's back, and were delighted to be on such intimate terms with the King of the Unicorns and the Duke of Wensleydale); Oswald himself, blue as a peacock's feather, ear trumpet at the ready; and Tabitha looking pinker than normal with excitement. At the big banqueting table at one end of the room sat what Simon called the High Command. There was H.H., Parrot and Dulcibelle, Ethelred, Penelope and the boys. On the table in front of them was the model of Cockatrice Castle. When they were all assembled, Simon, who had been chosen as spokesman, rose to his feet, holding a long stick and banged it on the table for silence. Gradually, everyone stopped squeaking, whispering and rustling, and silence fell.

"Ladies and Gentlemen," Simon began, "I've been asked by H.H. to address you. You all know why we're here – our objective is to take Cockatrice Castle, teach the Cockatrices a lesson and, above all, to rescue the Great Books of Government."

At this there was a great cheer, stamping of feet and a clapping of paws and hooves and hands.

"Now," continued Simon, "the point is this. We have only one opportunity, so we must make no mistakes, that's why we're all gathered here, so that each one knows what he's going to do. The one thing we must prevent at all costs is the Cockatrices burning or destroying the Great Books out of spite, which – as you know – they're more than capable of doing. So our plan of attack must be one which will keep the enemy so busy he won't have time to think of destroying the Great Books until it is too late. Now, we have some idea of what the Cockatrices are up to, due to the bravery of two members of our group: First, Ethelred Toad here, who with incredible bravery and cunning disguised himself in a masterly way as an Indian snake charmer and made his way into Cockatrice Castle."

There was a chorus of "Ooos" and a burst of clapping, and Ethelred blushed.

"With the aid of a friend of his, who's a grass snake, he entertained the Cockatrices to some conjuring tricks and snake charming. He found out that, although the Cockatrices don't know *exactly* what we are up to, they know we are up to *something* and they're jolly nervous. Ethelred here, let off a firework, and he says they all ran round in circles, bumping into each other."

There was a burst of laughing and clapping.

"Early this morning," Simon went on, grinning, "our one and only *indomitable*, *inimitable* and *intrepid* Mr Parrot carried out a daring aerial reconnaissance of the Castle."

There were cries of "Bravo" and "Three cheers for Parrot", and much clapping. Parrot bowed to left and right.

"H swooped down low over the battlements and was able to see the Cockatrices have several cannons in position and cauldrons of boiling oil as well. This seems to be their main defence. Apart from this, they seem to be relying on the moat and the great door to protect them. I may add that Mr Parrot flew down low over the sentries on the battlements and shouted 'Look out, look out, your doom is approaching.' Whereupon, I am delighted to report, two of them got such a fright they fell off the battlements into the moat."

At this there was a burst of cheering and much laughter.

"However," Simon went on, "although we may laugh, we must not underestimate our opponents. They are wicked, cruel and dangerous, but to show you how important it is that we win I want Ethelred to read to you a set of the new regulations that the Cockatrices are going to put into force when they're governing the country."

Simon sat down and Ethelred got to his feet, unrolled a parchment scroll and started to read:

"*Item 1*
All Phoenix to be banished from Mythologia, together with any Sea Serpent more than five feet long."

"Blasted nerve!" roared Oswald.

"*Item 2*
All Dragons to be used for pulling carts of heavy things, like building materials, for the Cockatrices."

"Cheek," said Tabitha, going scarlet with rage.

"*Item 3*
All Unicorns to have their horns cut off and be used to pull carriages for the Cockatrices."

There was a great whinny of anger and a clattering of horns and hooves from the Unicorns.

> "*Item 4*
> All Toads to be used for hatching Cockatrice eggs, scrubbing floors and serving at table in the Castle."

The Toads' eyes all bulged with horror.

> "*Item 5*
> All Mermaids to be used to pull boats and rafts for the Cockatrices, and to scrub out the moat round the Castle three times a week."

"The impudence! the impertinence! Scrub out *moats*, me, what's so well-connected!" said Desdemona in a fury.

> "*Item 6*
> All Weasels to be used as nursemaids, cooks, footmen, gardeners and so forth at Cockatrice Castle."

"Me? Duke of Weaseldom! A Cockatrice's *nurse*?" said Wensleydale in horror. "Me? The Cockatrices' *footman*."

> "*Item 7*
> H.H. to agree to work for the Cockatrices and to help them with the spells."

"*Never*," shouted H.H. "Never, never, *never*."
And everybody clapped and cheered.

> "*Item 8*
> Things to be encouraged:
>   An enormous increase in the number of Cockatrices, so that they may rule the country.
>   A steady increase in the number of Mandrakes, Werewolves and other sober, intelligent and likeable members of the community."

At this there was such a roar of rage and fury, such a turmoil and such a shouting it was like a clap of thunder. Wensleydale got so excited that he hit Winifred on the head with his gold-mounted cane, by mistake. Toads waved their pikes with such anger that several Weasels got black eyes, and four of the more sensitive Firedrakes fainted. It was a good five minutes before order was restored and Simon could make himself heard.

"Now," he said, "you see why it is so important we should win."

"Yes, yes," shouted everyone.

"Very well," said Simon. "Now, I'd like you all to pay attention while I tell you how we're going to attack and what each of you has to do."

Everybody watched eagerly as Simon pushed the model of Cockatrice Castle into the middle of the table where they could all see it.

"Now this is a model of Cockatrice Castle," he said, pointing with his rod "and, as you can see, it is shaped rather like a wedding cake, with a hollow centre and four towers. The hollow centre is the great courtyard. Here, around it, is the moat, and here is the drawbridge and the door into the Castle. Is that clear to you all?"

"Yes, yes, *quite* clear," said everyone.

"Well, this is how we shall attack," said Simon. "On the left and on the right of the Castle will be the Griffons with five catapults apiece. The gold cannon balls will be heated by Tabitha before firing, so that they will set fire to anything they land on, just to cause a nuisance. Now, as soon as the Griffons fire the *first* salvo a highly trained Toad, a cousin of Ethelred's, called Egbert (who's already in the Castle) will cut the ropes that will bring the drawbridge down. Unfortunately, on his own, he can't open the big doors, but as soon as the drawbridge is down the doors will be charged and broken down by repeated battering from my brother Peter's noble troop of Unicorn Cavalry. As soon as this is under way, two things will happen simultaneously:

1 Miss Williamson Smythe-Smythe-Browne and her young ladies, accompanied by our good friend Oswald, will enter the moat and pull out the great plug. The water level will start to go down.

2 At that moment, I, with a fleet of balloons driven by Firedrakes and with baskets full of Weasels, will take off, fly over the Castle and land in the great court-yard and on the battlements. Each Weasel will be equipped with fireproof clothing and a lavender-water pistol apiece. Their job is to fight and harry the Cockatrices as much as possible.

"Once the water level has dropped in the moat and exposed the drains, there will be two or three of them marked by Egbert with red flags. These are the drains that lead directly into the dungeons where the Great Books are kept.

"Now, a big group consisting of Weasels, accompanied by Penelope's Terrifying Toad Brigade, will make their way up the drains, overpower the sentries, and then stand guard over the Great Books until the Castle is taken.

"Now, is that all quite clear?"

Everyone said it was as clear as crystal.

"Right," said Simon. "I want you all in your positions at *exactly* six o'clock tomorrow morning, and *exactly* at half past six the Griffons will fire the first salvo. That's all, and good luck."

As they were leaving the great banqueting hall, Penelope went up to Ethelred.

"Ethelred, I think it was *exceedingly* brave of you to go to Cockatrice Castle like that and organise everything so wonderfully," she said.

"Oh, it wasn't nothing really," he said. "I told you me mastery over disguises was one of me best things."

"Well, I think it was very clever of you," said Penelope, "and now I'm going to ask you a special favour."

"Anything, anything at all, miss," said Ethelred, earnestly. "You just tell me and I'll do it."

"Promise?" asked Penelope.

"Yes, miss, of *course*," said Ethelred.

"Well," said Penelope, "you're going up the drains with the Terrifying Toads, aren't you?"

"Yes, miss," said Ethelred. "I'm leading them, like."

"I want to come with you," said Penelope.

"'Ere! No, 'old on a minute, miss," said Ethelred in a panic. "That's not *fair*, I can't take you with me, 'onest. If anything happened to you I'd never forgive meself, and neither would anyone else."

"A promise is a promise," said Penelope. "I'm not just going to *sit* here while everyone else is *doing* something. I must come with you, please Ethelred. I'll wear one of those nice, red uniforms and pile my hair up under the hat, so that no one will know. I promise to do exactly what I'm told and you'll protect me."

"Blimey, miss," said Ethelred, miserably. "If any of the others should 'ear of this, they'd skin me, 'onest they would."

"Then you'll do it?" cried Penelope.

"Well, I promised, didn't I," said Ethelred. "So, I suppose I'll 'ave to. Only, please miss, do take care, won't you, because it won't 'alf be dangerous."

"I'll take great care," Penelope promised.

Parrot had chosen to be General Overseer over the whole battle, and he was to fly round and round the Castle, supervising the action generally and taking reports back to H.H. who, in his private balloon, was to be tethered at a vantage point where he could see what was going on.

So at ten minutes to six the following morning H.H.'s balloon slowly rose into the sky at the end of its long, silken rope, especially spun for H.H. by Dulcibelle. H.H. was armed with a lavender-water pistol, just in case, a large packet of sandwiches, a bottle of Moon-carrot gingerbeer, and Parrot's telescope. Parrot perched on the side of the basket, ready to fly off when the battle commenced. From his basket, swaying up in the sky, H.H.

could see Cockatrice Castle far below and watch the movement of his troops.

On the dot of six, the Griffons manoeuvred their catapults into position, and a battalion of Weasels placed neat piles of cannon balls by each one. Tabitha ran from pile to pile, heating them up with her breath until they glowed and almost melted.

In the meantime, the Weasels, Toads, Mermaids and Oswald had concealed themselves in the Cork forest near the edge of the moat. And behind a small range of hills opposite the drawbridge Peter had drawn up his Cavalry and Simon had all his balloons tethered.

All was now in readiness, and they waited patiently, and a bit fearfully, for H.H. to give the signal. At half past six precisely, H.H. leant out of his basket and waved a large, green flag with gold stripes, which was the flag of Mythologia, and the battle for Cockatrice Castle began.

Eight Griffons using their long ladles loaded the golden cannon balls on to the catapults. Eight other Griffons, at a signal from their leader, pressed the levers and the catapults went off, shooting the golden cannon balls, glittering and whining, through the sky to crash into the battlements of the Castle, where they lay smouldering while the Cockatrices rushed about with buckets of water trying to put them out. After three salvos, the top part of the battlements was nearly in ruins and many parts were on fire, and the Cockatrices were so disorganised that it was obvious they were taken unawares. However, they did manage to drag several of their cannons into new positions and fired a few rounds at the Griffons, but their aim, unlike the Griffons', was bad.

As this was happening, the great drawbridge suddenly fell with a crash, like thunder, and they knew that Egbert, the Toad, had successfully cut the ropes. Immediately, Peter, in his handsome blue and gold uniform that Penelope had made specially for him, blew the charge on nis trumpet. A hundred and fifty Unicorns in lavender and white came over the brow of the hill, shoulder to shoulder. At first they trotted, then, as they neared the wide drawbridge, Peter gave an order and they formed a column of four. Another order and they changed from a trot into a canter and then from a canter into a gallop. Nostrils wide, horns flashing in the rising sun, they galloped down towards the drawbridge.

As the first wave galloped on to it, their hooves sounded like thunder on the wood, and then there was a splintering crash as their horns dug themselves deeply into the great, wooden door. Wave followed wave of Unicorns, thundering across the drawbridge and crashing into the door which slowly, but surely, was starting to splinter and fall to pieces under this onslaught. Desperately, the Cockatrices dragged some of their huge cauldrons of boiling oil to the edge of the battlements above the drawbridge and poured them down. Parrot, circling just above, would shout a warning, and the Unicorns would leap out of the way, as the oil splashed and bubbled on to the drawbridge. Then a picked body of Weasels, carrying buckets, ran on to the drawbridge and scattered sand and gravel over the oil, so that the Unicorns would not slip.

As the first wave of Unicorns galloped across the drawbridge, Oswald carrying Desdemona and her young ladies on his back, riding side-saddle, made his way out of the Cork forest and down to the moat. Seeing what a large target he was, the Cockatrices trained their cannon on him and fired again and again. Cannon balls thudded into the ground all round Oswald, hissing through the air and ploughing up the purple grass, but, miraculously, neither he nor Desdemona and her group were hit. They reached the moat safely and submerged beneath the water.

As they did so, from behind the hills Simon's aerial

attack started. The transparent balloons, glittering all the colours of the rainbow with the Firedrakes inside them, rose into the sky, and, dangling beneath each, was a basket full of infuriated Weasels. The Weasels had, in fact, drunk so much rue that Simon had had great difficulty in preventing them from fighting *each other* as they waited for the signal to take off. As the balloons drifted over the battlements furious Cockatrices spat great gulps of flame at them, but they were too far away. However, the Weasels retaliated by bursts from their lavender-water pistols, and they soon had the Cockatrices on the battlements gasping and coughing and reeling about with streaming eyes. One of them, in fact, sneezed so hard that he fell into a cauldron of boiling oil and got severely burnt. Gradually, the balloons with their cheering cargo of Weasels floated over the battlements and started to descend into the great courtyard.

In the depths of the moat, meanwhile, Desdemona and the young ladies had found the great plug. It had been hard to find, because they only knew approximately where it was, and it was covered with sludge and slime, so they could not see it at first. They discovered it at last and attached a rope to the ring in it; then with some difficulty attached the rope to Oswald. The problem was that when they tried to tie the rope round Oswald's chest, he, being exceedingly ticklish, giggled so much that he had to come up for air. In the end, they had to fasten the rope round his neck. Then with Oswald and all the Mermaids pulling, they managed at last to get the great plug loose. There was a great glup of muddy water, and H.H. watching through his telescope, saw a whirlpool form over the plug and there was a whoosh and gurgle like a giant bath being emptied, and the water level in the moat started to go down rapidly.

The Cockatrices were thoroughly muddled by so many different attacks, but they still fought on grimly.

Cannon balls from the Griffons continued to thud into the battlements. The great doors of the Castle had been almost cut to pieces by the Unicorns' horns. Simon's balloons had just landed in the great courtyard and the Cockatrices were being attacked by blood-thirsty Weasels with lavender-water pistols.

Then the last of the water gurgled down the great plug and the moat was bare and muddy. Sure enough, in the Castle walls there could be seen numerous drains like the one the children had used to enter the Castle before. At the mouth of two of these hung red flags. This was the moment that Commander-in-Chief Ethelred had been waiting for. He led his fifty eager and indignant Toads, that made up Penelope's Terrifying Toad Brigade, and his so blood-thirsty Weasels out of the Cork wood and down to the moat. They were all armed with fireproof shields and lavender-water pistols. Penelope, looking very smart in her red uniform and feathered hat, ran beside him.

"Please, miss," panted Ethelred as they scrambled down into the muddy moat and started to squelch their way across. "Please, miss, stay close to me and don't do nothing dangerous."

"All right, I promise," said Penelope, her face flushed with excitement. "Isn't this *thrilling*?"

"Cor blimey, no it isn't," said Ethelred, as a cannon-ball splashed into the mud beside them. "It's too dangerous to be thrilling."

They reached the marked tunnels, and here Ethelred divided his forces into two. Urging upon them all the need for absolute silence, so that they could take the sentries by surprise, he sent the Weasels up one drain while he and Penelope led Penelope's Terrifying Toads up the other. To Penelope, scrambling along in the gloom behind Ethelred, it seemed the drain would never end. Then, suddenly, in front of them was an iron grille and beyond it the corridor which led to the dungeons where the Great Books were hidden. Carefully, they removed the grille and the Toads crept through into the corridor. A little farther up the corridor another grille had been removed and the Weasels were pouring through that. They joined forces with the Toads, and led by Ethelred and Penelope they made their way silently up the corridor.

Peering round the corner, Penelope and Ethelred could see that there was a group of about ten Cockatrices who had obviously been left to guard the Books, and who were grouped at the bottom of the stairs, arguing. It was plain that they did not think they could be attacked from the rear, for they were arguing as to whether or not they ought to go up and join the fight in the great court-yard. Eventually, their leader decided that one of them would stay and set fire to the Great Books, if necessary, while the others went up and joined the fight. So they opened the door of the dungeon in which the Great Books were and the Cockatrice took up his stand by them, ready to blast them with flames. The rest of them clattered up the stairs to the courtyard.

"What are we going to do?" whispered Penelope. "If we all rush down the corridor he's going to see us and set fire to the Books."

"Yes," said Ethelred. " 'Elp me out of me uniform, miss, quick."

Quickly, Penelope helped him out of his uniform and then, before she could stop him, he hopped round the corner and down the corridor towards the dungeon, carrying his lavender-water pistol.

" 'Ere," shouted Ethelred to the sentry. " 'Ere, you, sentry, where's all the others, then?"

"Don't come any closer," warned the Cockatrice, "or I'll blast you with flame."

"Wot's the matter with *you* then?" asked Ethelred. "I've

just come to bring you and your Chief an interesting bit of information, I 'ave. Look at this 'ere."

Ethelred waved his lavender-water pistol at the sentry.

"What's that?" asked the sentry, suspiciously.

"I just found a Weasel down one of them drains," said Ethelred, "and I 'it 'im on the 'ead with a rock. 'E was carrying one of these. These are the things wot the Weasels are knocking your lot out with up there. Deadly they are. I'm not quite sure 'ow they work though."

Ethelred had stopped just outside the dungeon door and was fiddling with the pistol, as though he really did not know how to use it.

"Here, give it to me, I'll take it to the sergeant," said the Cockatrice, and he stepped away from the Great Books and into the corridor. As he did so, Ethelred squirted a jet of lavender-water straight into his beak. Immediately, the Cockatrice reeled backwards, gasping and coughing, sneezing out great sheets of flame. Penelope knew that this was the moment and she turned to the ranks of Toads and Weasels behind her and shouted "Charge!" and then ran down the corridor with the animals hopping and scuttling behind her.

The Cockatrice, seeing this mass of the enemy descending on him, turned to run, and immediately fifty jets of lavender-water from the pistols of fifty Toads hit him, and another fifty followed from the pistols of the Weasels. The Cockatrice uttered a strange, gulping cry, twisted round several times and fell unconscious on his beak.

"Quick," said Ethelred. "Ten of you Weasels, ten of you Toads – in there to guard them Books."

As soon as they were safely in the dungeon, Ethelred locked them in and gave Penelope the key.

"Now, you stay 'ere, miss," he panted. "Me and the rest are going upstairs."

So saying, he led the rest of the Toads and Weasels up

the staircase and into the courtyard. Here, the fight was almost over. Half suffocated by the lavender-water the sneezing Cockatrices were being herded into bundles by the triumphant Weasels and tied together. Seeing that he could do nothing very helpful, Ethelred left his Toads and Weasels to help in tying up the Cockatrices and went down to the dungeons again. At the bottom of the steps he stopped in horror.

Penelope, standing outside the dungeon door, was unaware that the Cockatrice had regained consciousness and was creeping towards her, its eyes alight with fury. Ethelred looked round desperately, for he was unarmed. Luckily, lying on the floor was a pike which had been dropped by one of the toads. Picking it up, Ethelred took careful aim and hurled it, so that just as the Cockatrice was going to blast Penelope with a sheet of flame he was hit between the eyes by the pike and fell senseless to the floor.

"Oh, Ethelred, you saved my life," said Penelope, shuddering as she looked down at the fallen Cockatrice, smoke and flame dribbling from its nostrils.

"Think nothing of it," said Ethelred, modestly. "You saved *my* life, miss."

Now great cheering broke out in the courtyard, and over the drawbridge rode H.H. on the King Unicorn. He passed under the battlements, scarred and battered by the Griffons' barrage, through the tattered remains of the gate split to bits by the Unicorns, and into the courtyard where the sad groups of wheezing Cockatrices were under guard from the Weasels and Toads. He stopped in the centre of the courtyard, and from the dungeons came a procession of Penelope's Terrifying Toads, carrying between them the three Great Books of Government on their gold and silver stands. At the sight of them, safe and sound, such a cheer went up that it could be heard all over Mythologia.

Then the King of the Unicorns, carrying H.H., set off towards the Crystal Caves; and Penelope and the Terrible Toads followed behind, carrying the Great Books, and behind them came all the Unicorns, the Griffons, Oswald and the Mermaids, Tabitha proudly carrying her basket of eggs, and all the Weasels and Toads, while above them flew balloons full of Firedrakes. So, with this triumphant procession the Great Books of Government were returned to the Crystal Caves and the safe-keeping of Hengist Hannibal Junketberry.

There is not very much more to tell. H.H. banished the Cockatrices to a remote island in the Singing Sea until they had learnt to be respectable creatures again. Cockatrice Castle was to be repaired and given to Oswald to start a restaurant in, which pleased him immensely. *All* Tabitha's eggs hatched out in due course, making sure that there would always be Dragons in Mythologia.

The day the children were leaving, H.H. arranged a special farewell and thankyou lunch for them. This took place on a beach by the Singing Sea, and several great tables were arranged, stretching out into the water, like piers or jetties, so that the sea creatures could sit at the sea end, and the land creatures could sit at the land end. It was a magnificent banquet cooked especially by Oswald, and many speeches were made and toasts drunk. At the end, H.H. made a speech.

"Dear Penelope, Peter and Simon," he said. "It is through your kindness and your intelligence and your bravery that Mythologia was saved. We are sorry to see you go, but you know that you will always be welcome to come here at any time in the future."

At this there were great cries of "Hear, hear."

"And now," continued H.H., "from us all I'd like to present you with this gift."

H.H. handed a beautifully carved box to Penelope, and when she opened it she gasped. Inside were three necklaces for herself – one of pearls, one of rubies and one of diamonds. There were also pearl, diamond and ruby cuff-links, and tie-pins for Peter and Simon. Finally, there were the three decorations – the Order of the Cockatrice. These showed a fallen Cockatrice and all the the other creatures of Mythologia triumphant in the background. The decorations had been beautifully executed in minute precious stones, seed pearls and gold and silver filigree work. The whole box was like a treasure chest, and the children were overwhelmed. Everyone seeing their delight, burst into "For they are Jolly Good Fellows" and Penelope found that her eyes were full of tears. Finally, they embraced all their friends and, last of all, H.H.

"Come back soon," he said. "We shall be looking forward to it."

"We will," the children promised, "we will."

Then they mounted on three Unicorns and Ethelred and Parrot mounted on a fourth, to see them off, and they rode away, leaving all their friends happily continuing the party by the shore of the Singing Sea.

After an hour's stiff gallop they arrived at the same entrance by which they had entered Mythologia.

" 'Ere, miss," whispered Ethelred, as they dismounted. "Could I 'ave a word in private with you?"

"Of course," she said, and she followed him behind the rocks.

"I was wondering, miss, if you'd do something for me like," said Ethelred blushing.

"Anything Ethelred, you know that," said Penelope.

"Well, it's like this," said Ethelred, getting redder and redder, "I was . . . reading this 'ere story once about this 'ere Toad, see, and then there was this er . . . princess, see, and she sort of kinda . . . she well kisses the Toad like, and, cor lummy, he turns into a 'andsome prince."

"So, you want me to kiss you?" asked Penelope.

"If you ain't a princess, I've never seen one," said Ethelred earnestly. "So, if you wouldn't mind, miss; I mean just once, as a sort of experiment."

"Of course," said Penelope.

So Ethelred closed his eyes tightly and Penelope leant forward and kissed him.

"Cor lummy," said Ethelred, his eyes still closed. "Is there any difference, miss?"

"I'm afraid not," said Penelope.

Two big tears squeezed out of Ethelred's eyes and slid slowly down his cheeks.

"And I am very *glad*," said Penelope. Ethelred opened his eyes in astonishment. "Glad, miss?" he said. "Why?"

"I don't want you as an awful, handsome prince," said Penelope. "I want you as the handsome, brave and kind Toad that you are."

"Cor, miss, you really mean that?" asked Ethelred, beaming. "'Onest, cross your 'eart, and spit on your 'and and 'ope to die?"

"Honest," said Penelope. And to show that she meant it, she kissed him again.

"Come on, Penny," yelled Peter, "or we'll never get home."

They went to the mouth of the tunnel. There the two boys shook Parrot's claw and Penelope kissed him on both sides of his beak.

"Good-bye, my kind, brave and dear friends," said Parrot. "Please come back soon."

"Yes, as soon as possible," said Ethelred.

"We'll try to come back next year," said Penelope. "We promise. We'll send you a message through Madame Hortense."

The children took one last look at Mythologia with its beautiful blue forests of cork trees and the purple grass, the glint in the distance of the golden Singing Sea and the jade-green sky with its families of coloured clouds. They looked once more at their friends, Ethelred and Parrot, and, behind them the lavender and white Unicorns nodding their heads in farewell. Then, with a final wave of their hands, Penelope, Peter and Simon plunged into the tunnel that was to take them back to the everyday world.

The Phantom Tollbooth

NORTON JUSTER

'It seems to me that almost everything is a waste of time,'
Milo remarks as he walks dejectedly home from school.
But his glumness soon turns to surprise when he unwraps
a mysterious package marked ONE GENUINE PHANTOM
TOLLBOOTH. Once through the Phantom Tollboth Milo
has no more time to be bored for before him lies the strange
land of the Kingdom of Wisdom and a series of even
stranger adventures when he meets the watchdog Tock
who ticks, King Azaz the unabridged the unhappy ruler
of Dictionopolis, Faintly Macabre the not so wicked Which,
the Whether Man and the threadbare Excuse, among a
collection of the most logically illogical characters ever
met on this side or that side of reality.

For readers of ten upwards.

The Third Class Genie

ROBERT LEESON

Disasters were leading two nil on Alec's disaster-triumph scorecard, when he slipped into the vacant factory lot, locally known as the Tank. Ginger Wallace was hot on his heels, ready to destroy him, and Alec had escaped just in the nick of time. There were disasters awaiting him at home too, when he discovered that he would have to move out of his room and into the boxroom. And, of course, there was school . . .

But Alec's luck changed when he found a beer can that was still sealed, but obviously empty. Stranger still, when he held it up to his ear, he could hear a faint snoring . . . When Alec finally opened the mysterious can, something happened that gave triumphs a roaring and most unexpected lead.

A hilarious story for readers of ten upwards.